I0702837

PRINT EDITION

THE PHEEWORKER'S OATH© 2024

by Mirror World Publishing and Adam Gaylord
Edited by: Robert Dowsett
Cover Design by: Manthos Lappas

Published by Mirror World Publishing in March 2024.

Mirror World Publishing

Windsor, Ontario
www.mirrorworldpublishing.com
info@mirrorworldpublishing.com

ISBN: 978-1-998360-01-7

THE PHEEWORKER'S OATH

Adam Gaylord

mirror world publishing

For my wife. You're my everything.

THE PHEEWORKER'S OATH

"Survivors." I pointed across the debris-strewn clearing to a tangle of timber and metal where phee, the natural power that flowed over my world, the Great Egg, swirled the faintest semi-transparent blue-green. There was a subtle difference from the strands around it and only an experienced healer, such as myself, would have noticed.

Hassan whistled and a half-dozen humans converged on the pile.

"Careful." I stepped between two females to crouch down and peer under a timber bearing deep claw marks, extending my tail for balance. While I couldn't see the humans trapped within, I could tell by the flickering of the phee that flowed through the pile that their situation was dire. "Move slowly. They're badly injured."

Hassan's people shifted the debris as gently as they could manage. Like most dwellings in the various human settlements, the structure had been cobbled together with parts of their downed spacecraft, held together with what they call adobe—bricks of dried red mud mixed with straw. This home had been small and took little time to dig through. With a grunt, the largest male tossed aside a hunk of what had been their ship's outer hull, exposing a tangle of human bodies.

I crawled forward to kneel by the motionless forms.

Hassan crouched beside me, his brows pinched. "They're alive?"

Humans can't see phee. Hassan had once told me their home planet—that most planets—don't have anything like phee. I think it is more likely humans can't see phee and are therefore unaware of it. The thought of a phee-less world, so cold and dead, made my tail tingle. Regardless, Hassan couldn't see how the flowing strands of semi-transparent color and light, as delicate as frost on a leaf, failed to interact with the humans atop the pile, an adult male and a female, both with dark brown skin and black hair, presumably mates.

"Help me move them," I instructed.

Together we rolled the bodies aside, exposing two adolescent females, both unconscious. I rested my hand against the back of the oldest, the deep brown smoothness of her skin contrasting with my light blue scales. Closing my eyes, I stretched out my consciousness, coaxing a thin tendril of turquoise phee from the flow around us. With a subtle hand gesture, I willed the tendril into the small of her back, traveling with it through the alien anatomy that had grown so familiar to me. I kept the phee insubstantial to pass through bone and tissue rather than to manipulate or cut. From her tailbone, I guided the strand around the curve of her pelvis before traveling back up through the spine, minute changes in how the phee interacted with the girl's body setting my path.

"Broken hip, broken vertebra," I listed the girl's injuries. I could bind the broken bones, and at her age she would heal quickly. The general anatomy of a human was curiously similar to that of an Atipok, each species composed of mostly the same organs and bones of similar shape and placement. Similar but noticeably different, like a drawing by an artist who'd been told about an animal without ever actually seeing it.

"Ruptured spleen," I continued. That would be a bit trickier but might be survivable if addressed quickly. "Broken ribs." I winced. "Punctured collapsed lung, massive internal bleeding." I leaned back, withdrawing the phee and my hand. A moment of fatigue washed over me. Manipulating phee in such a precise fashion was always draining. "I'm sorry. I can't save her."

Hassan touched my arm and I opened my eyes. "Takey, are you sure? Can you try?"

I managed to suppress a hiss of anger. Although he was human, I considered Hassan a friend. He was a craftsman of some sort before their arrival, and many humans now looked to him for leadership.

He also embraced phee as useful, even if he didn't understand it or shrink from its use in fear like so many other humans. But friend or no, I didn't appreciate having my judgment as a healer questioned.

"I'm sorry," he added quickly. "I didn't mean anything by it. I'm just frustrated. This—" His gesture took in the whole of the wreckage that had been a community only the previous day. Two men were lining up bodies next to their mechanical wagon. Like the other attacks, I suspected some remains would never be found, having been dragged away or completely consumed. His eyes settle on a row of claw marks gouged deep into the soil. "This can't keep happening."

Chatraka, the huge apex predators of the southern grasslands, rarely strayed this far north. In their native range, attacks were rare, and only upon lone travelers, but this was the third attack on a human settlement in as many lunars. Something had changed.

Of course, since the humans had crashed into our planet, much had changed.

I exhaled, my anger dissipating, and moved on to the younger female. She lay on her side, apparently unharmed, shielded from violence by her familial cocoon. I rested my hand on her shoulder and harnessed another tendril of phee, willing it into the center of her limp form.

The phee tendril blunted and bent like a piece of straw thrust against the side of a wagon.

I flinched.

"What's wrong?" Hassan asked.

"Just a moment." Again, I tried to coax power into the girl, this time more subtly, much as I would for one of my own kind. Medical pheework is invasive by its very nature. Insinuating phee into another without permission is an attack and a grievous crime amongst Atipok, second only to forcibly coercing a pheeworker's ability. As a healer, I'm allowed such intimate contact, but only with great care. Over the solars, I'd grown used to rougher treatment with my human patients given that they couldn't sense phee one way or the other.

On an Atipok, one of the easiest entry points is the tip of the tail. I figured the vestigial human tailbone might be an equivalent. I closed my eyes and traveled with the strand, attempting to gently needle it into the base of the girl's spine. Just as before, the strand deflected, not upon her skin, but upon a thin layer of elemental power that lay just on top, like a coating of liquid armor.

My scales rippled in surprise. My eyes swept the forest surrounding the clearing, the light blue needles of the pines swaying in the light breeze, but found no sign of outside manipulation. My mind raced as I tried to come up with some kind of explanation, but I quickly conceded there was but one.

I leaned back. "Fascinating," I murmured, as much to myself as Hassan.

"What? What's wrong?" Concern creased Hassan's broad face. Like all his kind he was rather ugly, but in a kindly sort of way. He had brown skin, although much lighter than the girl's, with short cropped black fur circling his face.

"Who is this girl?" I asked.

"I think her name is Molly. Her parents are—were—Sam and Monica."

"How old is she?"

"I don't know, twelve or thirteen. Why?"

I glanced at the other humans standing around us, watching the scene. Several eyed me with suspicion, a common reaction to pheework among humans. A couple looked downright hostile. Hassan caught on and dismissed them to look for salvageable provisions. Then he turned back to me. "Okay, what's going on?"

"This girl is the first known human pheeworker."

"What? Are you su—" He hesitated. "I mean, how is that possible?"

"I don't know."

"Well, is she okay?"

"She's encased in phee."

I felt around her head, checking for lumps, unsure of whether her shield would contain a fracture. I tried and failed to lift an eyelid, and had similar luck opening her mouth. With care, I was able to roll her gently onto her back, but my fingers were met with physical resistance when I attempted to feel her abdomen. All I could do was lower my head to her chest, counting her heartbeats and listening to her breath.

I sat up. "She seems fine, but I can't be sure."

"You can't see into her?"

"No. She's blocking me." I didn't revel in admitting a human child's pheework was giving me trouble, but thankfully Hassan didn't react. "I think I can get around it, but I might damage her without help."

"Help?"

I nodded. "I see no physical reason for her to be unconscious. I suspect she's trapped within her own shield. Barriers like the one she is using are mostly instinctual. If I simply muscle my way through it, I might seriously damage her unconscious mind. I need support from other healers."

Hassan stroked his chin fur. "When can you get someone here?"

"Not for some time, I'm afraid. Atalan starts in three days. All Atipok are called to Salitat." The annual sacred gathering held in our great stone capital city was not to be missed. "I leave tomorrow. Once Atalan starts, none will leave until it ends."

"Crap. How long will Atalan last?"

"Many days. It's impossible to know for sure."

"Can she wait until it's done?"

I looked the girl over, then shook my head. "Setting aside the very real chance of death by dehydration, she's more than just physically trapped. She's trapped within her own mind. Unless her parents were secretly pheeworkers, which I doubt, then she's had no training. She needs a guide to coax her out of her own head or she might destroy herself." Small bumps arose on the girl's naked skin. I pulled a blanket from the nearby debris and draped it over her. The poor thing was just a nestling. I couldn't help but feel bad for her, which might explain why I didn't take the time to consider the implication of my next words. "There is another option. I can take her to Salitat and get her the help she needs."

Hassan's thick eyebrows arched skyward. "I didn't think humans were allowed in Salitat."

"They're not," I conceded, equally surprised by my offer. "It will be a risk." That was an understatement. Anti-human sentiment had been increasing. To bring a human to Atalan could easily be construed as treason. I would be putting us both in danger. "But I don't think she has any other options."

Hassan sighed, massaging his temples with one large, calloused hand. "Very well, I'll pull together a few men and we'll—"

I help up a hand. "No one else. Only the girl."

"But I can't let her go alone," Hassan protested.

"She won't be alone."

"You know what I mean. I can't just let you take her."

"Then she will stay, and she will die." I didn't like being so blunt with Hassan. He was a caring man and a good leader, but the situation was grim. I shouldn't have made the offer in the first place and there were no other options.

I could see conflict play on the human's features. He looked around, like he was searching for another way. "Crap," he said finally. "Gimme a minute." He stomped off in the direction of his people.

I watched him, mulling over another consideration I hadn't shared. In the thirteen solars since their crash landing, other than some initial hostilities and the Battle of the Red Plain, humans and Atipok had managed a tenuous peace. We mostly kept to our own, them in their adobe villages, us in our stone cities. But there were a few individuals, such as myself, who worked to bridge the gap. I felt it was my duty as a healer to help them. I'd taken an oath to do so. And over time I'd developed a certain respect, even a fondness for their ways. But my time with them had also revealed their tendency toward violence. They loved their weapons. I rarely saw an adult human who wasn't carrying a plasma pistol or rifle. Even now, Hassan carried one of each, a pistol on his hip and a rifle across his back. Such things were unknown to us before their arrival and while they were no match for skilled pheework, humans still managed to kill each other on a regular basis. I sometimes wondered how readily they would abandon their makeshift towns in favor of our great stone cities if not held at bay by their fear of phee. If this girl represented a new trend, if humans gained the ability to pheework, it would completely change the balance of power between our species.

I had to present this girl to the queen.

Hassan returned looking no less frustrated. "I asked around and nobody seems to know if she has any other family. Her group's been on their own for the last couple years, really sticking to themselves. She's all alone now." He looked down at the girl. "My guys think I should decide but…"

"You think it should go before the council," I finished for him.

"Unfortunately, yes."

To call the human's system of organization and decision making an actual government was a bit too generous. Every group seemed to have their own leader or leaders, Hassan among them. And, like Hassan, some actually followed the general rules set out by the charter of their spaceship, which he explained to me at one point. Of course, other leaders had their own ideas. The general disorganization was something I didn't understand but Hassan assured me had to do with the human desire for freedom and independence. To me, it just looked like chaos.

There were times, though, when a decision had to be made and that decision abided by all humans. This fell to their council, a group of as many of the various leaders as they could gather. I had limited experience with the council but to say they were wary of Atipok, and with anything involving phee, was optimistic. Some were downright hostile.

I glanced at Dulkat and Galt, the twin suns, then over at Aesop, my old dolk, grazing on a nearby patch of sweetgrass. Hassan said he looked like an oblong haystack with legs, his long black fur sun-stained yellow after too many solars pulling my wagon. I'd named the herdbeast after the author of my favorite human fable, the tortoise's slow and steady approach mirroring both my own philosophy as well as my dolk's usual pace of travel.

"It's mid-morning. I need to leave tomorrow before first light, with or without the girl."

"I'll send a runner ahead." Hassan signaled a nearby female. "We'll be lucky to make a quorum, but we'll have to make do."

I wasn't sure what that meant but I nodded anyway. "Hassan, I don't know what you told your people, but I suggest…discretion on the matter of the girl's phee abilities."

"I can't lie to the council," he said simply.

"Then don't. Tell them the truth. Tell them that I am a healer who needs help to treat a serious ailment. Tell them without that help, she will die. Leave it at that."

He cocked his head. "You don't think we humans can handle the idea of a human pheeworker?"

My eyes flicked briefly to the pistol on his hip. "Do you?"

He returned my gaze for a long moment, then turned to instruct his runner.

It was dark by the time our caravan rolled past the first of the sparse shacks that marked the edge of the largest human settlement. Centered on the remains of the Hawking, the humans' massive, downed spacecraft, the town had been known by many names during its short life. I gathered that most of them, like Babylon,

Avalon, and New Mecca, had some sort of religious or mythical origin. Eventually, practicality and ease of reference had won out. Nowadays, the ever-growing sprawl of adobe shacks was known by most as Shiptown.

A pair of females with plasma rifles greeted us near the outskirts, informing us that the council was already assembled. We hurried down the main thoroughfare, me in my dolk-pulled wagon and the humans on foot. Or rather, Hassan urged us on while Aesop plodded along at his usual languorous pace. A long row of solar powered lamps lit the way. Spherical helmets salvaged from spacesuits—clothing that allowed the humans to walk amongst the stars, or so I'd been told—served as lampshades, their orange tinted visors casting a warm glow in the cool evening air.

Shiptown was unusually quiet, the main thoroughfare nearly deserted. Normally a returning party would be met with laughing children and hearty handshakes. Instead, males and females waved from the entrances of their adobe homes, children held back by firm hands. Aesop snorted in his reins, the furry herdbeast responding to the tension in the air.

"It's the gryphon attacks," Hassan answered my unasked question, using the human name for the chatraka, a reference to some mythical beast of the human home world, which apparently resembled the noble apex predator of our southern plains. Hassan had shown me a picture of an eagle and another of a lion, and explained a gryphon was an amalgamation of the two. I found the comparison distasteful.

"They have everyone on edge, especially those on the outskirts."

Up ahead a raucous pack of children burst from a side street and charged straight for us.

I smiled. "Not everyone."

We slowed as Hassan's four sons mobbed our party. Mahira, his wife, trailed close behind, her long purple robes skimming the deeply rutted road. His youngest, little Ahmed, whom I had helped birth, secured his favorite perch atop his father's broad shoulders while the oldest, Yasin, scratched behind Aesop's ear, eliciting a happy hum from the old beast. The other two chased one another around my wagon, one growling and the other giggling.

"Stay close," Mahira scolded the runners before turning to me. "Healer Takey." She gave a slight bow. "Welcome."

I returned the bow, noting the tension around her eyes, and how when she greeted her husband they embraced a little longer than usual. I found the signs disconcerting. Mahira was probably the most level-headed human I knew. If she was on edge, as Hassan put it, that didn't bode well for the mood of the rest of the settlement. Humans were unpredictable at the best of times. Riled up, they could be dangerous.

Mahira and the children walked with us. I noted that the former seemed to make a particular effort to smile and wave to the families along the route. It dawned on me that the presence of Hassan's family meant more than I'd initially recognized. It was a show of strength, a signal to the other residents of Shiptown that they shouldn't be afraid.

When we approached the center of town, Hassan's family left us, Mahira shepherding her brood back in the direction of their home. We soon neared the Hawking, a seemingly endless tower of small, circular, evenly spaced portholes lit from within. Even though only half the ship had survived the crash, the scale of the remains never failed to fill me with awe. Nearly half a million humans had lived and died for generations in its ancient hull as they crossed distances that I couldn't comprehend. I'd been told it was only one of seven such ships—and the smallest among them at that—to escape their dying planet. Each having gone their own way, the rest might still be out there searching the stars for a home.

Or not.

We made our way through an increasingly dense crowd to the brighter lights of the town square, a decidedly non-square shaped clearing to one side of the Hawking where the humans held community events. As reported, the stage on the side of the square nearest the ship already held the long table used for council meetings. Four human leaders, two males and two females, sat on the far side of the table, watching our approach with varying levels of interest. I knew them all, having worked in each of their communities at one time or another. There was Dolly, a short pale plump female who caught my eye with a smile. Milan, a male with a preponderance of orange facial fur and a manner of speech I found hard to follow, leaned to the side and said something to Elisha. The tall, dark-skinned female with no fur on her head didn't acknowledge whatever passed between them except to scoot her chair a little further away. The fourth human that had managed to make it in time, I was disappointed to see, was Chan, commander of the human militia. He sat hunched over the table, glaring at us with a scowl so intense that I wondered if he was trying to frighten us away.

I looked around, spotting Chan's son, Mau, off to one side of the stage. The lanky adolescent gave me a hesitant smile. The shell had fallen pretty far from the egg with that one. Mau was shy, soft-spoken, and surprisingly curious about pheework. I'd treated his broken arm a few solars back and he'd asked a number of intelligent questions. He'd claimed the arm was the result of a fall, but I saw he flinched whenever his father walked into the room and the yellowing bruises on his ribs. I hadn't pushed the matter. It wasn't my place. I gave Mau a minute nod.

We stopped before the stage and a hush fell over the crowd. The proceedings started without preamble. Hassan presented the situation just as I had advised, a sick girl that needed care she could only get by going with me. Two human healers carried her into the Hawking so that they could perform their own examination. The council asked a few questions, mostly about the chatraka attack, and I stayed quiet, more than happy to let Hassan do the talking. I noticed that Chan did the same, at least until Hassan moved to take the matter to a vote. Suddenly Chan was on his feet, his chair toppling backward with a loud clatter. He would have towered over us without the stage. Humans are generally larger of frame and stature than Atipok, but even among humans Chan was large. On stage, he seemed a true giant.

"Are you seriously suggesting that we send an incapacitated child alone to lizard city?"

I let out a low hiss. Chan was perfectly aware how we felt about the L-word.

"You know we'll never see her again," he said flatly, like it was an indisputable fact.

"Of course we'll see her again." Hassan's tone was soothing. "Whether he can help or not, Takey will bring her back."

I had agreed to no such thing, but I knew humans were strangely particular about their dead. I made a mental note to talk to Hassan about volunteering my time but otherwise didn't react.

Chan scoffed. "You believe that? Where does this trust come from? From years of them letting us rot in our scrap pile while they sit comfortably in their stone mansions? A trust born from working our fingers to the bone while they use their black magic to stifle our growth at every turn? How do we know this girl isn't under some spell? Maybe this so-called healer used his dark phee to knock her out just to get her back to their capital unprotected."

"Enough!" I growled, my frustration boiling over.

Chan glared at me in triumph. "I must have hit pretty close to home." He righted his chair and sat down.

I returned his glare, seething. Chan was far from the only human who resorted to blaming his every frustration on Atipok and phee, but he was probably the most vocal. Even on the few occasions when I'd been allowed to help members of his community, the visits had been tense, closely monitored, and his thanks afterward laced with half-insults and insinuations. His accusations were dolk manure, but his followers had been steadily growing in numbers for solars.

I disliked him.

"I do trust Takey," Hassan spoke up. "For years I've trusted him with the lives of my people, of my family." He paused, his eyes scanning the faces at the table. "And I know you have too. Why would we abandon that trust now?"

Elisha stood. "Takey has earned my trust and my respect." She turned to me with a small bow, which I returned. "But sending one of our own, one of our children, to the forbidden Atipok capital, it goes beyond trust. There are too many uncertainties, chief among them what we would do if, for reasons beyond his control, Takey isn't able to return the girl. Would we leave her? Or are we prepared to march on Salitat to get her back?" She visibly shuttered at that proposition. "I need more of an assurance."

Milan nodded and Chan looked triumphant.

The proceeding was momentarily interrupted by the return of the human healers. Their report was much as I had expected, that the girl was in some kind of coma and that their medical scanners had failed to determine a cause. They departed after declining to give an opinion on whether I should be allowed to take the girl. As they walked away, Hassan caught my eye, my solid light green to his white with a brown ring, my vertical grey pupils to his centered black circle. His expression was difficult to read. Was it pleading? Or regret?

Before I could reason it out, he turned back to the council. "Takey can give the assurance you need," he told Elisha. "It's called a 'life oath'."

A heavy weight seemed to settle upon my shoulders. Over the solars, Hassan and I had shared many things, some of those things in confidence, the deema, or life oath as he called it, chief among them. I had never betrayed his confidence and until now, and as far as I knew, he hadn't betrayed mine. But this…this was not only a betrayal to me but to all Atipok. Although unseen by the humans, phee boiled at my feet, responding to the anger coursing through me.

"You and I will talk," I hissed quietly.

Without turning his head, he gave a minute nod. "The Atipok take their promises very seriously," he continued to Elisha. "More seriously than many humans I've known. Breaking an oath can mean ostracism or even death among their kind. But Takey can go even further. He once told me, in a confidence that I now break, that as a healer he has a way to bind the phee to his promise such that if he breaks it, he will die."

A murmur swept through the crowd.

I noted his carefully chosen words and my anger abated, if only slightly. He'd publicly admitted wrong and apologized, in his way. And he'd made it sound like deema were a providence of healers and not all Atipok. Of course, we would still have our talk.

Elisha turned her attention to me. "Is this true?"

I could deny it. As Hassan had just shown, lying was so commonplace amongst humans as to be unremarkable. Sometimes I think they almost expect it. At the moment, however, behaving in any way like a human held a certain revulsion. "It is."

"And would you do this?" she asked.

Chan made an exaggerated gesture of confusion. "So we're supposed to trust that we can trust him? How's that any different?"

Elisha ignored him. "Takey, will you take a life oath to return the girl to us, and to help her in any way you can until you do?"

The attention of every human assembled turned to me. I stared ahead, seeing nothing. I thought of the girl, an alien trapped by a power she should never have been able to touch. But also no more than a nestling, and doomed if I didn't help her. I thought of the need to get this girl to the queen and the threat of phee-wielding humans. I thought of the chance to prove Chan and his kind wrong and the bridge that might be built if our people could learn to use phee together. Finally, I looked at Hassan, a liar and a fool, and my friend.

I closed my eyes, gesturing with my fingers as I plucked a thin tendril of shimmering gold from the flow at my feet and guided it up my tail, then through my body to the ancient part of my brain, the controller of breath and heartbeat. With a flick of my hands, I bound the strand and then stretched it tight, binding the other end to that place in me, the part of my brain that understood the very essence of the words that I spoke. "I will save the girl if I can. And if I can't, I will bring her back to you. I give you my life oath." The phee snapped into a quivering taught bowstring of power I knew I would feel every moment until I fulfilled the deema and it was discharged, or until I broke my oath and the bowstring snapped through my brain like a steel blade. The phee wasn't bound to any action, necessarily, but rather to my belief in my actions. To fulfill my oath, I had to believe that I was truly doing everything I could for the girl. Any doubt, any attempt to lie to myself, the oath would be broken, and I would die.

The council members gathered briefly, except for Chan who stayed in his seat. Then one by one they gave their vote, again Chan the outsider, the others agreeing to send the girl with me to Salitat. To the side of the stage, I saw Mau give an approving nod before fading back into the crowd. Hassan thanked the council, Chan not even letting him finish before storming offstage.

Then Hassan turned to me. "What can we do to help you on your way?"

I left before Galt, the first sun, broke the horizon the following morning. The girl lay covered in a blanket behind my seat, just another bundle in my wagon to anyone who didn't know better. Aesop lumbered along at his slow but constant pace. The old herdbeast was nearing the end of his days and I suspected this would be his last trip to the capital. We'd been together a long time and I didn't look forward to the haggling I'd have to do to barter for a new dolk. My stocks were running low. I was going to have to come up with some tradables if I wanted to avoid pulling the wagon myself.

I couldn't help but feel a buzz of excitement to be on the road. No matter where they're hatched, every Atipok has but one true home: the great stone city of Salitat. Phee only flows over and through living stone and soil. You can bind phee to yourself to accomplish small workings when off the ground, like when I bound phee to a broken bone to keep it in place and help it heal, or like the girl seemed to have done with her thin shield. I kept a little phee with me while up on my wagon, for example. But to do anything meaningful, a pheeworker has to be connected to the Great Egg.

All the world is one big egg, inside which lives the Great Mother of all Atipok, the dream weaver, who is connected to her children via the phee, using it to gather and store the collective memories of all Atipok. Phee is an extension of her will, alive but not an animal, conscious but not sentient. The red stone pillars, arches, and structures of Salitat were carved from the living stone, rather than just constructed upon it. Every part of Salitat is part of the egg, connected to the Great Mother, and rich with phee. It is the home of all Atipok and I hadn't set foot in its walls in a solar, since last Atalan.

I also looked forward to the simple pleasure of being around other Atipok. Humans were decent enough, most of them, and I generally enjoyed my time with them. But they weren't Atipok. Everything they did, even the most closely shared customs and practices, were flavored with oddity, with approaches or perspectives I couldn't completely grasp. I suspect it had as much to do with their phee-blindness as it did with their place of origin. The difference left me perpetually on guard, even around humans I trusted, who were few and far between. It would feel good to be amongst my own people again.

There was one Atipok in particular I hoped to see.

As I rode, I probed at the girl's shield, more to take my mind off the ever-present throb of the deema than in any real hope of cracking it. I hadn't told Hassan, but it was unlike any pheework I'd ever seen. Phee changes color as it interacts with the world. As a healer, I was specially trained to detect very subtle shifts in color that might mean any number of things when phee interacts with a patient. The phee that flowed over the land, parting around the thick, furry legs of my dolk and swirling in eddies behind the wagon, shifted from the yellows and oranges of earth and plants to greens and blues of sentient species. All the phee I'd ever seen glowed in the myriad of colors of light shone through a crystal; no white or black but everything in-between. The shield surrounding the girl though, the color of the phee she subconsciously willed around her, was white, pure bright white like new fallen snow. I'd never seen white phee. It was light before the crystal. I hadn't thought such a thing possible.

Actually, the seamless barrier of white encasing the girl reminded me a little of an Atipok egg, although I cringed inwardly at associating anything human with the purity of state that was an eggling. The human birth process is primitive and disgusting in comparison, closer to a dolk's. An Atipok egg is perfection embodied. Its round wide base tapers to a rounded conical point, reminding us to aspire to greatness while maintaining our hold of the now. Every egg is identical, reminding us both of the first egg, from which we all descend, and that we are all one people. The shell is strong yet fragile, much like our lives.

It was that underlying fragility of the girl's shell that sparked the comparison as much as the color. There was strength in the girl's phee, no doubt about that. And a shield is the easiest, most intuitive, and therefore the strongest pheework a body can do. But I'd worked with some of the strongest pheeworkers alive. I'd even once had the honor of channeling the queen. A careless dolk had stepped on a hatchling's tail in the market, crushing it badly. I was set to bind the bones when the small crowd around us parted and Queen Phallat, who had been on a tour of some kind, stepped through and offered to support my work. It was a gesture of goodwill and an honor, so of course I accepted. If she'd recognized me, she gave no indication. I opened myself and she funneled more phee into me than I'd ever worked with in my entire life. Cumulatively. I was able to heal the multiple fractures so completely that I didn't even need to bind residual phee to the bones for support. The crowd had applauded, and the queen had departed with a courteous nod to my deep bow. I'd like to think she remembered me.

This girl didn't have anything like that kind of power, but the shield did have strength. It was so different, so alien, that although it was still phee, I couldn't figure out how to interact with it. So engrossed with my attempts was I that I didn't notice Aesop stray from the path until he stopped. I came back to myself to find us parked in a thicket of tall sweetgrass, Aesop humming with pleasure as he chomped big mouthfuls of green.

I took a breath to scold him, but only chuckled, deciding he had the right idea. I retrieved a jar of dried fruit from behind my seat and was prying off the lid when I heard an unfamiliar gurgling rumble.

I stood, scanning the horizon, only to realize the sound was coming from below.

"What's wrong with you?" I'd never heard the old dolk make such a noise.

Aesop swung his head low from side to side, the grumble gaining volume.

I strained my neck to peer down at where he'd been grazing. "Did you get into a patch of crazy bush? What's…"

As silent as the phee, a chatraka emerged from the swaying grass. She was young, her wide, serrated beak still stippled. And she was big, longer and taller than Aesop. She paced only a couple wagon-lengths away, so close that I could see powerful shoulder muscles rippling under her short golden fur.

I froze, my mouth suddenly dry. Images of the splintered remains of the girls' town flashed through my mind. For all I knew, this could be the very chatraka that had killed the girl's family. My hands shook.

The great beast paced back and forth, head bobbing in and out of the phee that flowed past Aesop to swirl around her feet. Chatraka and dolk, both of the southern plains, one predator and the other prey, were the only animals known to sense phee, although they couldn't interact with it.

But I could.

Slowly, I stepped down off my wagon.

The chatraka squawked.

I braced for its charge, my legs almost giving way with fear, but the beast resumed its pacing. With a deep breath, I planted my feet and gathered phee, holding back the flow until it built up around my waist and then my shoulders. My toes burrowed into the soil and my jaw clenched as I strained to hold the wave back. A moment before it toppled me, I released the wave with a growl. A small tsunami of pent up phee sped toward the chatraka, breaking upon the beast with a rainbow spray of power.

The mist settled to reveal the chatraka, standing just as it had been. She snorted in an unimpressed sort of way.

I shrugged at Aesop. "It was worth a shot."

I flinched as the chatraka squawked again, gouging furrows in the soil with her huge talons. She reared onto her hind legs, peering over my head into the wagon. Did she smell something? One of my healing herbs? Or perhaps the human? Or maybe she could sense the white phee, a phenomenon as alien to the creature as it was to me.

Regardless, she seemed to decide something. She dropped to all fours, gave the wagon one last look, gave me one more snort, and turned to fade into the sweetgrass.

My head swam and I gripped the wagon for support. I was used to very subtle and precise pheework. That inelegant wave had left me more tired than I had any right to be.

"I'm getting too old for this."

I managed to climb back up into my seat and eat a few strips of dried fruit, which helped. While I chewed, I tried to remember the last time I'd used offensive phee. Certainly, I'd been tempted only the evening before. In the end, my talk with Hassan had been only that, a talk. I knew he was only trying to care for his people. His betrayal, although disappointing, wasn't malicious. Not that I planned to share secrets with him or any other human anytime soon.

It occurred to me that the last time I'd even been prepared to use offensive phee was the Battle of the Red Plain, the decisive clash between humans and Atipok that had defined the roles of each race and their interactions ever since.

I leaned back to rest and thought about that day thirteen solars ago.

It was a red day.

The aliens marched on Salitat, and we marched to meet them. From remote farms and small villages to the great stone city itself, Atipok fell into formation to protect our capital. As we marched, each footfall kicked up a puff of red dust from the dry barren plain. The combined steps of the amassed thousands coalescing into a veritable sandstorm, the light from the twin suns at our flank casting a red hue on the already red procession, each and every Atipok wrapped in the crimson silks of war. And at our front, our queen, perched on an intricately carved red litter.

I marched behind that litter, or rather behind Lakey, my mother, who marched behind the litter. It was a place of honor, my mother was the queen's healer and a trusted advisor, and me her apprentice.

I kept my eyes on the powerful arc of my mother's tail, an elaborate braid of red cloth weaving around its length, and tried to ignore the knots in my stomach. I kept telling myself that I should be filled with pride in the might of my people or righteous fury at the harms the aliens had inflicted. But in reality, I was just scared. I'd never worn my red silks and had never wanted to. I aspired to heal, like my mother. I was no soldier.

Of course, few who marched were soldiers. Generally, only a small standing army kept the peace in the capital. The Atipok hadn't seen war in generations. It was the aliens, the hew-mans, as they called themselves, that drove this conflict. We hadn't known peace since their massive vessel crashed from the stars in a firestorm of death and destruction. I had been out with friends that night not two lunars before and had been granted a stunning view of the fall of the enormous starship, watching in awe and horror as it broke in two and plunged into our world. One half had stayed intact enough to shelter the humans we now marched against. The other half had broken up and plummeted into a village, killing all that lived there and strewing debris for leagues across the plain across which we now marched. Columns of Atipok snaked around hunks of twisted charred metal that had once sailed amongst the stars. I looked down and saw the remains of some kind of small animal, buttons sewed where its eyes should be and white fluff protruding from a tear on its side.

"Takey," mother scolded in a whisper. "Get back in formation."

I looked up and realized that I'd drifted out of line. I fell back into step immediately behind her, one of the queen's guards eyeing me with disapproval. It wasn't long before we crested a low hill and the main hull of the broken half of the spaceship came into view. What once must have been a grand structure was now a gigantic heap of smoldering metal, beams and columns poking every which way like the broken bones of some giant wrecked bird. The human army, smaller than our own but still tens of thousands strong, hunkered in formation around the ruins. They'd marched for days from the more intact half of their ship. Somehow it seemed fitting that the armies now met at the crash site of the other half of their crippled vessel. Scattered amongst their ranks loomed a half dozen glowing columns, otherworldly weapons we knew nothing about. My stomach clenched at the sight of them.

Queen Phallat held up a hand and our troops ground to a halt. Red dust rolled forward across the plain, briefly obscuring the opposing army. When it settled, I saw a handful of humans had broken from the rest and were marching forward under the banner of a black flag sporting a blue and green orb. The queen gave a nod and several Atipok broke rank, my mother among them, moving forward to intercept the humans.

The two groups met only a few hundred paces in front of the queen's litter but despite the heavy silence that had engulfed the plain, I couldn't make out what was said. Of course, given how little each species understood of the other's language, I doubted those in the actual meeting were faring much better. A short time and a lot of exaggerated gestures later, the groups split and my mother and the rest returned. Before she fell into rank she caught my eye, the corners of her own crimped with worry.

The dolk herder who was serving as an interpreter stepped before the queen's litter. He had cared for several injured humans immediately after the crash which, for better or worse, made him the closest thing to an expert we had. He shifted back and forth on his feet. "Pha Phallat," he addressed her with a nervous bow. "They want us to step aside. They mean to take Salitat."

The queen's eyes narrowed. "Do they? On what grounds?"

"I think they plan to settle there. They made it pretty clear that they think they can destroy us but that they don't want to." He looked as uncomfortable with his report as I felt. "I think they want to take Salitat and then negotiate a truce from a position of strength."

"How much of that did they tell you and how much is speculation?"

"Equal part of both, pha," the interpreter admitted with a shrug. "Communication is still difficult, at best."

The queen didn't reply. In silence we waited. The heat of the twin suns warmed my scales, my stomach clenched in anticipation. I glanced at my mother but her stance betrayed nothing. Across the plain the humans were equally still. The only movement was that of the phee. It flowed between the armies, churning and bubbling in fiery oranges and yellows, aggravated by the marching thousands and the threat of violence. Finally, the queen spoke. "We will not surrender our home," she said simply.

The interpreter bowed and backed away before turning and striding out into the plain. At the same time, General Jakka, the commander of our forces standing to one side of the litter, raised his hand high. A pair of Atipok broke rank and took position in front of the formation, phee boiling around them. The interpreter unwound a length of silk from his arm before waving it in the air. It must have been some mutually agreed upon signal because the human's response was immediate. The glowing columns that had been the focus of so much speculation ratcheted slowly down to point in our direction. At the same moment, the general dropped his hand and the pair of Atipok each shot three quick bursts of deep violet phee straight up into the air.

I recognized the signal as one of the few orders I'd ever managed to memorize: raise shields. In response, the leading edge of our force gathered the phee churning at their feet and cascaded it skyward in a wall of fire-tinted translucent power. From the humans' side, a low, throbbing hum broke the silence and one of the now horizontal pillars pulsed in time with the increasing cadence and pitch of the hum. I winced as the pulsing hum sped to a sharp staccato vibration. The soldiers around me glanced nervously at one another and I caught my mother's eye. She gave me a small nod of encouragement.

Almost as if her gesture had been some kind of cue, the vibration jumped octaves into a piercing scream and a bolt of white-hot plasma rent the air between the two armies, slamming into the shield paces in front of the queen's litter. Atipok shrank back, recoiling in fear as the plasma crackled and danced across the face of our shield. Sparks flew and the smell of burnt ozone filled the air. I squatted in place, squinting at the tentacle of energy as it lashed at the barrier, reaching for our queen.

And then, just as suddenly as it appeared, the plasma bolt was gone, the scream of the weapon replaced with a heavy silence. Across the plain, smoke rose from the now dull pillar as humans scurried around it like sugar bugs around fallen fruit.

General Jakka turned to the queen.

She raised a hand. "Hold."

Those Atipok that had dived aside resumed their places. I stood, equal parts relieved and confused. Was that it? Was that all the mysterious human weapons were capable of?

In answer, the other five columns started to pulse and hum just as the first had. Moments later they joined in a deafening scream as once again, tongues of energy lapped at our defensive shield, their fire again concentrated on the queen's litter. This time everyone managed to hold their ground. Even my own shaky knees succeeded in keeping me upright. And just as before, the plasma beams didn't even manage to push our shield back.

I glanced around, noting expressions of relief and a few smiles. A soldier near me even chuckled until her commanding officer quieted her with a reproachful look. I felt my tail droop a little in relief but when I looked to my mother she seemed just as tense as before, her tail high, her focus still on the humans and their ineffective weapons.

The bolts vanished and silence once again reigned on the barren plain. All was still for a long moment. Then a low murmur arose from our side.

"Is that the best they got?" a voice behind me asked.

"There must be more," another voice answered.

"Maybe the phee is different on their world. Maybe those things can bust through," speculated the first voice.

"Sounds like their phee is weak," scoffed another voice.

Queen Phallat raised a hand and the chatter died away, the sound replaced by the low rumble of thousands of marching feet. The humans were advancing.

Whatever relief I'd felt at the failure of their weapons vanished at the site of the alien horde bearing down upon our position. The ground shook with the force of their advance, huge shiny machines on rolling tracks adding to the thunder of tens of thousands of footfalls. And as they marched the humans chanted in their strange tongue, "For. Earth. For. Earth. For. Earth."

I had no idea what it meant but the booming bass of it filled me with a terror I saw mirrored on the faces around me, on every face except that of the queen. She sat in her litter unmoved, stoic in the face of the alien advance. Jakka looked to her but still she sat firm, the human army closing in. It wasn't until they'd cut the distance in half that the queen gave a nod and the general began barking orders. The casters pulsed phee up in an intricate dance of signals that I immediately gave up trying to interpret. My place was behind my mother. I took my orders from her.

Other Atipok, however, responded in a wave of action that rippled across the front, regional commanders filtering orders to the five squadrons. I caught a strand of phee from the dust at my feet and launched it skyward, casting my vision along with it to watch as squadrons carried out their assigned duties. The squad to our left forged phee into a series of hulking pestles, each poised several wagon-lengths in the air, ready to descend and grind anything they encountered against the mortar of the barren sandy plain. Rows of the glowing columns spread out and hovered a couple hundred paces in front of the shield. The squad to our right crafted phee into razor sharp pikes, each two or three times the length of a tail, and arranged them pointed outward in staggered rows between the shield and the hanging pestles. The squads flanking the ends of the formation maintained the shield while our squad, the center of the formation, waited for orders, ready to launch targeted attacks against specific threats.

Like a colossal, barbed gulper fish set to ambush its prey, the Atipok army waited for the approaching alien horde, who in contrast to our open display of power, hadn't so much as touched the phee boiling at their feet. I watched the wall of humans near, my anticipation growing with their every step, expecting them at any moment to unleash some hidden pheework, a devious attack or defensive shield, or at the very least pull up short of our fortifications.

They didn't stop. They didn't pheework. They advanced. They advanced right under the hanging pestles. They charged to within a dozen paces of the pikes, until most of their force was within range of our armaments. Then, with a nod from General Jakka and a flurry of signals, the slaughter started. Phee pestles dropped and rose, pounding out a staccato rhythm of destruction. Explosions raked the plain as their shiny machines were reduced to flaming piles of flattened debris. Alien cries of pain and confusion filled the air. The humans who made it past the pestles ran headlong into the pikes, almost as if they welcomed the razor-sharp death that pierced their hides. Red blood stained the already red plain.

I cut my phee tether loose, my sight returning to my eyes, my stomach churning. Gasps and cries of disbelief sounded around me, barely audible over the horrifying cries of anguish coming from the field of battle, although it could hardly be called a battle. I looked to my mother, whose expression was one of abject horror.

"They don't see it," she said to no one, her wide eyes on the humans.

I stepped toward her. "What?"

She glanced at me. "They don't see it. Our defenses. The pikes, the pestles. They don't see them. They can't. They're pheeless."

If it had come from anyone but my mother, I would have dismissed it. Lacking the ability to see or interact with phee is extremely rare. Maybe one or two Atipok in a generation are so cursed. The pheeless usually die as hatchlings, their condition just one in a suite of ailments cutting their life short. But a few survive, whole enough to live their lives, or whatever life one can expect without phee. They are a reminder that, while pheework is the birthright of all Atipok, it can't be taken for granted. Such individuals are sacred, in a way. They become wards of all Atipok. They are welcome anywhere and cared for with every diligence. It is the Atipok way.

But for a whole species to be pheeless, it didn't seem possible. "Are you sure?"

Rather than answer, she broke rank, heading straight for the queen's litter.

A guard stepped in front of her, bodily barring her approach.

"Pha Phallat!" she shouted over the guard and the cacophony of slaughter.

The queen turned her head and her eyes met my mother's, widening for the briefest moment. She nodded to the guard who stepped aside.

Mother stepped up to the litter. "Pha Phallat," she said after a deep bow. "The humans, they're pheeless. They can't see our defenses."

The queen glanced at the slaughter of the plain, then back to my mother. "Are you sure?"

"As sure as I can be. It's the only thing that makes sense."

The queen sat up and surveyed the horror before her. A long moment passed, one punctuated by the uninterrupted staccato of the dropping pestles and the chorus of alien death. The moment stretched on, the queen ridged in her litter, mother gazing up at her longtime friend. My heart felt as if it would burst from my lower torso if something didn't happen, but still the queen remained motionless.

"Please, Phallat," mother finally pleaded, dropping the honorific. "They're helpless. This is our first contact with a race from beyond our world. Will we destroy them? Will we wipe them out?"

Queen Phallat closed her eyes and then, with a deep breath, raised her hand. Signals burst and the pestles stopped, returning to their ready position hanging above the gore below them. She made a slashing motion and both the pestles and the pikes dissipated, leaving only the shield. What few humans that were able began a scurried retreat, dragging those that weren't. The howling from the plain lessened, even if only a little.

Mother bowed deeply, her nose nearly brushing the red soil at her feet. "Thank you, pha," she said.

The queen didn't acknowledge her and she backed away, falling back into formation and catching my eye for a brief moment before resuming her station.

My chest swelled with pride. I could only marvel at my mother's courage, to stand up to the queen, and her compassion, risking so much to try to spare a species she knew nothing about. I snapped to rigid attention, my tail and chin high, just like hers. Then and there I promised myself that someday, I would make that kind of difference to my people.

Dulkat, the second sun, was just starting to dip below the horizon when I finally reached the great rufous stone arch marking the entrance to Salitat. Beyond the wall towered the famous pillars and domes of the capital city, a dizzying array of geometric structures carved from the living stone itself. Banners of every color streamed from the tip of every spire, painting the sky with an array of color to compliment the spectrum of phee flowing over every surface.

I waited patiently as the flow of travelers bottlenecked, advancing a tail length or two when the opportunity presented itself while making sure my impatient dolk didn't trample anyone. I was relieved to be near the end of my journey, but I hadn't been in the throng long before an uneasiness tickled my scales. I brushed it aside but as we continued slowly forward, I became increasingly aware that something was off. It took me a few moments to figure it out.

It was quiet.

The atmosphere before Atalan was usually jovial. Atalan was a time for seeing old friends, making new ones, and finding mates. Not to mention all the trade. The streets would be filled with minstrels, bards, puppet theaters, phee weavers, food stands, and carts selling every kind of trinket or extravagance one could imagine. Some solars, the constant roar of the great city got so that sleep was hard to come by.

But even in a press of several hundred, I was pretty sure I could speak in normal tones and be heard at the back of the line. The mood was subdued, even grim. Even the phee seemed restrained, flowing glass smooth through the many legs and wheels of the throng. Travelers marched through the giant stone archway as if taking part in a human funeral procession. I wanted to chalk it up to weary feet and sore backsides, but the real reason was obvious.

Usually inconspicuous, brightly clad soldiers manned the great door, ringed the outer wall, and stalked along the ramparts of the great city in numbers I hadn't seen since the Battle of the Red Plain. They eyed the crowd like hungry krakka, the bands of crimson silk wrapping their arms and legs even more red in the light of the setting sun.

My deema throbbed as a soldier above me leaned over a parapet to scrutinize my wagon. I stole a quick glance behind me, partially reassured that the girl was still fully covered in her blanket. I suddenly wished I had thought to disguise her form a little more, but trying to do so now would only draw attention. Instead, I kept my head down like everyone else and passed through the huge carved doors into the capital.

The bluish glow of regularly spaced lamps revealed surprisingly empty streets. Atipok made straight paths for where they needed to go, not lingering or pausing to chat. I made my way past the business district and the financial quarter, and had almost made it into the healer's ward when a soldier stepped in front of my cart. Aesop gave an angry snort. He was tired and not in the mood for surprises. Neither was I.

The soldier raised a hand. "Hold."

My heart pounded in time with my deema as I fought to maintain composure. I slowed Aesop but didn't stop. "We've been on the road all day and my dolk is about to die on his feet so—"

"I said hold!" The soldier grabbed Aesop's reins, wrenching the animal to a stop. The dolk snorted and snuffed.

I stood, drawing myself up to my full height to tower over the soldier from my wagon. "Who do you think you are? On whose authority do you detain a healer for no reason?"

"Under my authority," said a voice from the other side of the wagon. I turned to see a second soldier, one I recognized. His name was Cordek, a low-level officer. Or at least he had been the last time I'd seen him. Now he wore the black banded crimson silks of a legion commander.

"Good evening, Commander," I said, trying to sound cheerful.

He sneered. "What's in the wagon?"

"I am a healer. These are my medicines and—"

"I know who you are, Takey. And you're no healer of Atipok. You're a healer of humans." The last word left his mouth as if it tasted bad. "Search it," he commanded a third soldier who had come up behind the wagon, joining the first. They started lifting up tarps and blankets, opening containers.

The deema twinged. "I'm a healer to all, Cordek. You know that. Do you remember that squad I put back together after you nearly tore them apart in training?" It was a hefty exaggeration. As I remembered it, Cordek had always been more of a talker than a doer, his gilded tongue getting him into trouble more often than not. But I hoped the fib might stroke the commander's pride.

Cordek straightened, looking pleased. "I remember. Good thing you were there to help." He glanced at his underlings, obviously hoping they'd overheard.

I glanced as well. The soldiers were working their way toward the front of the wagon where the girl lay directly behind my seat.

"But we still need to search your wagon," Cordek finished.

I shrugged. "That's fine, except for this bundle." I patted the blanket. The soldiers stopped.

Cordek's eyes narrowed. "Why? What's in the bundle?"

I glanced around and then leaned down, speaking low. "Phee fungus." Maybe I had spent too much time with humans. Their lying ways were rubbing off on me.

"Phee fungus?" He looked doubtful.

I nodded. "Very rare. It'll double your phee control. But it's very sensitive to light."

"It's dark," Cordek pointed out.

I hesitated but recovered. "Even lamplight."

"Then I'll look using phee."

"Invasive phee will ruin it," I stammered.

Cordek gave me a long look. The soldiers glanced at one another. "Search it," he told them.

My heart jumped into my throat and I was considering abandoning my wagon to make a run for it when a familiar silky voice emerged from the shadows on my side of the wagon.

"I'm sorry, Commander." Dalia glided gracefully into the lamplight. "It sounded to me like you just questioned the word of one of my most trusted healers."

Dalia was head of my order, nestmate to Queen Phallat, and one of the most powerful Atipok in Salitat. Not to mention that half the songs written over the last ten solars were about her beauty. Her scales glowed with iridescent blues and greens in the lamplight, accentuated by silks of similar shades. Her legs were thick and muscular, and her long lean tail curved a graceful arc over her head. She was the definition of femininity.

My scales rippled.

Cordek stiffened and the soldiers took a step back.

She smiled. "I must have misheard, mustn't I?"

Cordek looked like he'd swallowed a fire beetle. "Your most trusted healer just tried to sell me a pile of dolk manure about phee fungus."

"Phee fungus?" She shot me a look I knew all too well. Dalia and I had been close, at times. I even suspected that several of her offspring were of me, although obviously I had never asked. It was none of my business. My heart plunged into my abdomen.

"Did you explain how sensitive it is to light?" she asked.

I don't know who looked more surprised, Cordek or me, but I'd like to think I recovered first. "Not very well, I'm afraid." I shrugged. "I'm tired from the road and I think my explanation was…vague at best."

Thankfully, Cordek recognized the opening. "Unintelligible, really. Had you said it simply, you'd already be on your way."

"My apologies," I replied with a slight bow of my head.

"There." Dalia held out a hand. "Now, Commander, please help me up so I can guide my unintelligible healer to his rightful place."

That didn't sound good.

Cordek hustled around the front of the wagon only to be met by a low, gurgling rumble.

I flicked Aesop's reigns. "Quiet," I growled under my breath. The last thing I needed was my old dolk drawing more attention.

Thankfully, Cordek only squinted at the animal but didn't otherwise react, reaching Dalia to take her hand and help her up.

I slid over and handed her the reins.

Cordek dismissed the soldiers with a flick of his hand, his eyes meeting mine. "I'll be seeing you soon."

That didn't sound good either.

Dalia flicked the reins and the old dolk started forward with a lurch. When we were out of earshot I started to thank her, but she cut me off.

"Quiet," she growled.

We traveled the rest of the short wagon ride in silence. It wasn't until we'd pulled into a covered port and drawn the thick canvas flaps closed behind us that she turned to me.

"Phee fungus? Are you pulling my tail?"

I shrugged. "I panicked."

She shook her head. "And I always thought you lacked creativity."

"You did?"

She didn't respond. Instead, she walked to the back of the wagon and tugged aside the blanket. A sharp hiss and she fell back a hasty step. "Shells." She eyed the girl. "I should have let the soldiers have you."

I didn't think she was kidding. I quickly explained the situation, emphasizing my oath to heal Atipok and human alike and my intent to bring the girl before the queen, if she ever regained consciousness. Dalia didn't look happy, but she listened. When I finished, she stared at me so long that my scales started to crawl. Finally, she turned with a flick of her tail. "Bring it inside."

I gathered the girl in my arms and brought her into the healer's headquarters, carrying her upstairs to lay on a cot in a spare room. Dalia covered her with a soft blanket and we retreated downstairs. Someone had left out a plate of dried meats so I helped myself.

Dalia sat and poured herself a cup of warm blue dolk milk. "You couldn't have picked a worse time to pull this stunt. The attack outside Canant has left everyone on edge."

"What attack?" I said around a mouthful of jerky.

"You don't know?"

I shook my head.

"You really have been out with the humans too long. Takey, they ambushed a harvest party."

"Who did?"

"Humans. Three Atipok families were slaughtered. They had hatchlings with them. There were no survivors."

The jerky I'd been chewing suddenly lost its flavor. I swallowed dryly and set the rest aside. "How do we know it was humans? Plasma rifles?"

Dalia nodded. "The humans must have surprised them, killed them before they had a chance to defend themselves."

It didn't make any sense. The humans had kept their side of the peace for solars. Even that first decisive battle on the red plain had been more of a misunderstanding than a malicious attack. They'd somehow gotten in their heads the ridiculous notion that we planned to wipe them out. A "preemptive strike", they called their march. I'd always assumed they'd learned the harsh lesson of what happened to riflemen that go up against pheeworkers, but maybe not. Even so, I couldn't imagine Hassan or any of his people murdering hatchlings. I knew there were a few isolated groups with agendas. A couple were known for being pretty militant. But it had been quiet for so long. What had changed?

"Were they caught?" I asked.

"It was days before the families were even missed and days more before the bodies were found."

I grunted.

"Atipok are scared," Dalia continued, "and I can't blame them. Commander Cordek—"

I scoffed. "That stub-tailed jerk."

"Watch your tongue," she growled, glancing toward the door. I was surprised to recognize, perhaps not fear, but apprehension in her features. "Cordek has used the incident to push his expulsion ideas. He says we never should have allowed the humans to stay."

"Their ship was in pieces. How would they leave?"

"Doesn't matter. What matters is that more and more Atipok are listening to him. He hates humans and now he's commander of the legion. You couldn't have picked a worse enemy. He has soldiers everywhere."

That explained the greeting party at the city gate. "So what, we're supposed to kick them off the planet?"

She shook her head. "We're past that. Humans are unpredictable. And if they start to manipulate phee, like this girl, things will get ugly between our races, and fast."

It dawned on me what she was implying. "He's saying we should kill them? All of them? And you agree?"

She held up her hands defensively. "Hold on, I don't agree. I just…understand. I'm scared too. You know humans, but to the rest of us they're aliens who came here uninvited and have been causing trouble ever since. They're not like us and they can't be trusted."

I felt like I should respond. Part of me wanted to defend the humans I'd grown to appreciate. The rest of me couldn't disagree with what Dalia had said. I felt numb. In the end I just shrugged. "We have a little more than a day before Atalan," I said. "And we better have the girl conscious to present to the queen well before then. Can you help?"

She shook her head. "I have matters to attend to."

"But—"

She cut me off with a gesture. "I'll assign Landly and Hohonus. Besides you, they're the most familiar with humans. And I trust them."

I didn't know the healers, but I wasn't about to question her. "Thank you."

"Now go get some sleep."

I started to protest but again she cut me off.

"You're going to be useless as tired as you are. I'll have Landly and Hohonus here before daybreak." She stood and leaned over the table, resting her hand on mine. The sudden heartbeat pounding in my ears had nothing to do with the deema. "I probably won't see you again until Atalan," she said. "Good luck tomorrow."

I watched her go, wishing she wouldn't. The last I heard of her was a grumble from down the hall, "Phee fungus…"

"By the egg!" Hohonus exclaimed.

Landly fell back a step, eyes wide.

I had just pulled back the heavy wool blanket covering the still immobile girl, after warning the two healers that there was a human underneath it, of course.

Hohonus looked up expectantly at his bindmate. "Well?"

That the two were phee-bound was unusual for several reasons. The practice of using phee to bind oneself to a single mate for the rest of one's life had fallen out of favor generations before, but it was especially peculiar for these two. I had only just met my fellow healers, but the contrast was striking. The blustering Hohonus was so short and round that his head seemed to be actively sinking into his shoulders. Landly, on the other hand, was tall and lithe and moved about the small bedroom with the purposeful grace of a dancer. When the latter spoke, his words were measured and toned with a slightly aristocratic accent. Hohonus was brash and loud, his language as colorful as the phee itself.

Landly looked away, his nose high. "Well what?"

"Don't you 'well what' me you egg sucking dolk humper." Hohonus wagged a fat stubby finger a scale's breadth from Landly's chin, having to reach up above his own head to do so. "Say it!"

Landly sighed.

"Say it!" Hohonus repeated.

Landly turned to me with an expression of long-suffering. "Please forgive my companion. He has speculated on the existence of white phee for some time and seems to feel he's owed some sort of recognition."

"Good enough!" Hohonus beamed, appearing genuinely satisfied. "That's as close to 'you were right' as I'll ever get out of this one." He pinched at Landly's tail and the two shared an affectionate smile.

"To be fair," Landly chimed, "you've also been known to say that humans are too stupid to see phee, let alone use it."

Hohonus balked. "Why you stub-tailed—"

"Well," I said, cutting him off, "I've never even considered white phee. I doubt many have. Your speculation might make you the closest thing to an expert we have."

The healers' expressions sobered.

"The real question is," I continued, "have you speculated about how to interact with it?" I nodded towards the girl. "Because I haven't so much as dented her shield, and we're running out of time." I'd been up for hours before the other two arrived, poking and prodding the shield to no effect.

Hohonus rubbed thoughtfully at the dorsal crest on the crown of his forehead. The normally sharp spikes were worn down to nubs, hinting that the gesture was a habit. "It was really just a hunch. I just always figured that the Great Mother was up to more than we give her credit for. I mean, I've heard that the humans saw a whole scalin' other continent from space. One across the Green Sea. It's our scalin' planet and we didn't know about it." He shrugged. "What else don't we know?"

I'd been told the same by several humans, including Hassan. Still, the thought of an unknown land on the other side of the world was humbling.

My tail drooped. "Just a hunch," I echoed, unable to keep the defeat from my voice.

"Well now," Landly said, "the greatest things ever accomplished started from as much. I'd say we're in excellent company."

"That's right," Hohonus growled, opening the worn leather case of tinctures and balms he'd brought with him. "Don't count this pair of rotten eggs out yet. We've got a few tricks tucked in our scales."

I smiled, appreciating more and more the fire these two shared. "Okay then, let's get started."

Our efforts were cautious at first, each of us taking turns trying to insinuate, coerce, poke, prod, and otherwise disturb the girl's shield. Hohonus tried wafting various incenses into the girl's face in an attempt to stir her senses and draw her out. Landly wove intricate phee lacework to approach the shield from as many points as possible in an attempt to overwhelm it. I channeled the phee of the other two, melding it with my own to try to muscle through the barrier. It was during one of these latter attempts that we finally got a reaction, although not a welcome one.

"The poor dear," Landly said, the channel severed.

I'd felt it too, a wave of fear that rippled through her shield.

Every being that interacts with phee leaves their signature on it, their essence. Phee that was bound to an individual for a long time, like this girl's shield, could even transmit emotion, serving as sort of a conduit of the individual's state of mind. Although incapacitated, somewhere deep in the girl's unconsciousness, she was afraid.

I reestablished my connection, gently caressing a hand of phee over her shield while trying to project a sense of calm. The bound phee wasn't a one-way conduit. She could likely sense our efforts at some level. It seemed to help. The ripple abated.

After that, we continued with greater caution.

As our day progressed, I had the growing suspicion that our ever-lengthening list of failures had less to do with strength and skill and more to do with lack of understanding. We were trying to solve an algebraic equation with a song or hammer in a nail with strong rhetoric. There was some fundamentally alien aspect to how this human interacted with the phee that we couldn't understand.

It didn't help that we jumped at every shadow or breath of wind. I kept expecting Cordek to show up with a squad of soldiers for a "routine inspection". Landly, in particular, was so nervous that once, when a knock came at the downstairs door, he nearly fainted. It turned out to be a bone jewelry peddler, trying to drum up business by going door to door. Hohonus had to buy a rather hideous and entirely overpriced necklace just to get the persistent merchant moving and the door shut.

It was around midnight when I finally made the call. Landly stood across the girl's bed from me, swaying on his feet, his bloodshot eyes half-lidded. I could hear soft snoring coming from poor Hohonus, who had passed out an hour before and now resided in a chair in the corner.

"That's enough," I said.

Landly flinched. "What?"

"Go wake Hohonus and get yourselves to bed. Even if we managed something at this point, there's no chance we can see the queen before Atalan."

He hung his head, "I'm sorry, we—"

"No apologies. We've done all we can. You two acquitted yourselves admirably, and I'll be sure to pass that along to Dalia. You have my sincere thanks."

He gave a small bow and did as I had asked, Hohonus mumbling something about bone jewelry as they shuffled from the room, taking the lone lamp with them. I stood there alone in the dark for a while, not really thinking, just feeling frustrated and tired to the core of my bones. My deema was nearly silent. It was oddly reassuring. I truly believed we'd done all we could.

I don't know why, there were several open rooms just steps away, and I don't remember doing it, but when I awoke the next morning, I was spooned up next to the girl, my arm draped over her in a closeness I hadn't known with my own kind in many solars. Even after I gained awareness of my surroundings, I lay there with her for some time. We had failed, I had failed, and this girl would die. I guess I felt that a little support, a little protection in the same vein that her family had given her, was the least I could do. I stayed there until the bells chimed, announcing that Atalan would shortly begin.

When I left, I doubted I would see her alive again.

The Ovidium, the central structure of the capital city, was nearly full when I arrived, just a few stragglers trickling in. From the outside it looked like the top half of a colossal red egg, perfectly smooth and unbroken save for the dozen arched doors that ringed the ground level. I paused at one of the entrances to press my forehead against the living stone, its surface worn smooth by generations of Atipok that had done the same every solar since time began. The rock was warm, heated from within by molten magma running only meters beneath the surface. It was this liquid stone, back when the world was young, that had formed the enormous bubble that some distant ancestor had stumbled upon and subsequent generations had molded into our most sacred space.

I entered, taking a moment to wonder at the sheer size of the natural rock dome arching gracefully above the concentric rings of tiered stands in the great bowl below—the bottom half of the egg. No matter how many times I entered the Ovidium, it never failed to take my breath away. Nature, wielding the tools of water and time, had carved the great dome into a shining latticework of pearl-hued stone crosshatch, the intricate pattern punctuated with ominous-looking but stunning stalactites, the largest of which dwarfed the tallest of the stone towers outside.

Generations of our finest craftsmen had done their best to match nature's beauty with the bottom half of the bubble, the stadium whose steps I now descended. Lavishly carved benches of solid stone ringed the flawlessly smooth pearl floor. Every bench, every stair, every surface was embossed with impossibly fine reliefs ranging from flowers so real you could almost smell their sweet perfume, to great battle scenes featuring the heroes of our past. The Ovidium was a combined effort of nature and Atipok, just like the power that naturally accumulated there. Vast quantities of phee spilled out of the smooth pearl floor, flowing and churning in fountains of color up over the stadium and its inhabitants. I watched a hunt scene carved into the bench where I sat bubble with power, the stone figures ever locked in an epic chase seeming to come to life.

A hush came over the already reverently subdued thousands as a lone figure strode slowly out of the lone entrance to the stadium floor. She was wrapped in black silks, a stark contrast with the pearl floor which highlighted the rainbows of power dancing around her. Phee splashed up to tickle at her fingertips and swirled around her legs in loving caress, responding to our queen as it did to few others. She stopped in the center of the floor, right at the strongest upwelling, bowed her head, and, after a respectful pause, started to hum.

Atalan had begun.

In unison, the tens of thousands around her did the same, each lending their voice to the collective chorus. The sound soared, reverberating off the stone with a harmony I could feel deep in my chest. And with the sound soared the phee, every attendee taking up a strand and arching it up into the great dome, swirling and spinning around the central pillar of power that was Queen Phallat. Sound and phee danced together in the void, echoing and weaving in the traditional opening ceremony of Atalan, bringing us together as a unified people. There was no competition, no shameful attempt to outshine those around you. Every Atipok was part of the glorious whole with our beloved queen at our core.

I felt the stress and frustration of the last few days melt out of me, my deema all but a memory, reduced to a faint tickle by my certainty of failure. My mind soared with the phee I controlled as it weaved in and out of the multicolored fabric of my people. Joy at our combined strength and artistry coursed through me, heightened by awe of our queen's mastery. She was like an ancient tree, deeply rooted and unmoving while her hued leaves, we her Atipok, danced around her. The combination of colors and sound strained my senses joyously towards their breaking point, every awareness heightened.

Which is why the white-hot bolt of phee that blasted across the dome, tearing our fabric and scattering our leaves, nearly knocked me unconscious. I staggered, gripping the ornately carved bench for support. My sight returned to find the Atipok around me in similar states of shock. I tried to help the elder next to me up while looking around for the source of the attack. Cries of pain and anger rippled through the stands. Who dared to interrupt our most sacred rite?

Then I saw her, the human girl. She had come to the same entrance I had and stood wrapped in a blanket, the fur on her head disheveled. She looked scared.

The opening ceremony, I realized. That much phee, all of it inviting, all of it wielded an expression of free will and community, of course it would be an irresistible draw for a novice pheeworker. I should have known. You can't crack an egg lest you damage the hatchling. The only way is to draw it out.

Others must have seen the girl at the same moment for a furious roar arose from the stands. Some staggered back in fear while others charged forward. I should have stayed put. I could have melted into the crowd and been out of town by the time the soldiers realized how she'd gotten there. I was a healer. I knew edible plants and fungus better than most. I could live in the wilds. I could disappear.

Instead, I charged from my seat near the top of the stands up the stairs to where the girl stood. A sharp twang in the back of my head reminded me that my deema would have allowed nothing less. She may have been free of her phee prison, but she was far from out of danger and my deema knew it.

As I closed the gap, I reached out to her with phee. Every being that interacts with the phee leaves their signature on it, their essence. My hope was that she would distinguish mine, since I'd recently spent so much time interacting with her own. She saw me and a flicker of recognition hit her face just before I did, tackling her to the floor. I huddled atop her and clenched my eyes shut, waiting for the blows to fall.

I waited.

Nothing.

I squinted out one eye and then opened both wide in wonder. The girl and I were encased in a ball of power as white as the bolt that had disrupted the ceremony. Through it I could see the attacks raining down upon us, both physical and phee, but nothing got through. I recognized that kind of impenetrable barrier.

"You're doing this?" I asked, motioning with my eyes to the barrier.

Her wide eyes darted around the sphere, tears streaming down her face. "I think so."

I nodded. "Don't stop."

Moments later, the attacks ceased as suddenly as they had begun. I peered out through the white phee and saw the blur of a tall figure in black silks.

I swallowed. "Okay, you can stop now."

She shook her head, the motion quick and jerky.

"Ma…" I struggled for her name. "Molly, you have to trust me. I'm a healer. I help people, humans. Please, lower your shield."

Her features creased in strained concentration. "I don't know how!"

I chided myself. Of course she didn't know how. Had she been trained, we wouldn't have been in such a mess in the first place. I held up my hands, pressing my palms together. "Put your hands like this."

She hesitated, then did as I instructed.

"Your hands serve as a focal point. They give you something physical to concentrate on. Pretend that your shield is your hands, that they're one and the same." I gave her a moment. "Now release your hands and your shield." I drew my own hands apart.

She took a deep breath and copied my motion. The shield split and dissolved into its usual spectrum of colors, draining into the flow around us.

Queen Phallat towered above us, her expression unreadable. Cordek glared from over her shoulder. The queen looked at the girl and then at me. The Ovidium was silent.

Finally, she addressed us both. "Stand."

I guided the girl to her feet and we stood, the girl wrapped in her blanket, me straight backed and terrified.

She turned to the girl. "How did you get here?" she said in flawless human.

Molly glanced at me and I gave her a nod of encouragement. "I don't know," she said in a small voice. Then she asked, "Where are my parents?"

Queen Phallat glanced questioningly at me. I grabbed Molly's shoulders, turning her toward me. Our eyes were nearly level. "Molly, do you remember the chatraka, er, the gryphon attack?" I cringed inwardly to use the human word in front of my queen.

The girl withered. "They're dead, aren't they?"

I nodded.

"My siblings?" she choked.

"I'm sorry, Molly."

The girl collapsed against me, sobbing uncontrollably. I glanced nervously at the queen, but she seemed content to allow the girl a moment. I stroked the girl's bushy black fur and tried to imitate the cooing sounds I'd heard humans use to calm their young. Eventually she settled, although she didn't stop crying. Again, I looked to the queen.

"You're the healer from the market, the one who's been living with humans," she said matter-of-factly, switching back to Atipok.

Despite my fear, a surge of pride straightened my shoulders. She remembered me.

"Takey," I said, attempting an awkward bow while still holding the girl.

"You brought her here?"

"Yes, pha."

"Why?"

"Her family is dead. Her whole village, actually. And she was trapped inside her own phee. I couldn't get through to her, so I brought her to the healer's guild for help. My intent was to bring her before you if we succeeded, but we didn't. I thought she was doomed. I was going to take her body back to her people after Atalan."

"You brought a human to Salitat? During Atalan?" Her tone was flat.

I bowed my head, my eyes on the floor.

The queen turned back to the girl. "How long have you been a pheeworker?" she asked in human.

The girl looked confused. I spoke up. "The rainbows, Molly. How long have you been able to see them?"

She sniffed. "Oh, always, but nobody else can." She looked around. "Nobody else like me, anyway."

"And how long have you been able to touch them, to interact with them?" I asked.

"Not long."

"Why did you disrupt our ceremony?" the queen asked.

"I didn't mean to. It was just so beautiful and I wanted to make the rainbows fly, but all I can do is white." Her eyes suddenly widened. "Like the ball I made," she said to herself. "I could have saved them. I could have used that ball. But I didn't know how!" She dissolved once again into sobs.

Queen Phallat regarded her for a long moment. "I am sorry, nestling. I really am. But you cannot be allowed phee. No human can." She turned to me, continuing in Atipok. "Take her from here, find a way to sever her from the phee, take her back to her people," a cloud passed in front of her eyes, "and then report back to me."

She turned, her tail curled along her back to say that was her last word on the matter.

The deema throbbed at the base of my skull. During my training, I'd been told of a few instances when criminal Atipok had been forcefully severed from phee. It involved physically damaging portions of their brain. To say there were side effects was a significant understatement. As I understood it, the Atipok had been reduced to simpering idiots. As a result, it was widely considered more civil to simply execute criminals, which is why such a thing hadn't been attempted in generations.

"Please, Pha Phallat. Stripping her of phee will almost certainly damage her, and maybe kill her."

The queen didn't stop. "That's unfortunate." It wasn't a concession, simply a statement of fact.

"I can't harm her," I blurted. This time she did stop, although she didn't turn. The silence of the great stadium grew heavy upon me. I panted for breath, my mouth dry.

A guard stepped toward me with balled fists and a growl but stopped short at a flick of the queen's hand. "You would defy me?" Rather than anger, her tone was intrigued.

"Not willingly, pha." I attempted another bow, my voice shaking. "I don't have a choice."

She turned, a sharp gleam in her eyes, her head cocked in question.

"I've sworn a deema," I explained.

Queen Phallat looked me up and down, as if really seeing me for the first time. "You are a fool," she pronounced.

I couldn't disagree with her.

"You could still do as I command," she said.

"And die," I pointed out.

"Or do nothing."

"And die," I repeated.

She eyed me for a moment. "But there's more to it, isn't there? Why do you do what you do?"

Many a lonely night I'd spent among humans asking the same question. "Solars ago, my mother asked you to show the humans mercy. She did so out of a healer's respect for life, a healer's compassion."

For a moment, just the briefest moment, the queen's facade fell and I saw the sorrow and vulnerability of one who missed a friend.

Until that moment, I'd never known just how much my mother had meant to the queen. But before I could blink, the moment was gone, her regal countenance back in place. "You are of Lakey?" she asked with cool detachment.

I nodded. "I'm not half the healer, or half the Atipok she was, but I'd like to believe I share her ideals. I swore to protect this girl because I believe humans and Atipok can coexist. And because she's just a nestling, and I think my mother would have done the same."

I braced for a rebuke, that my mother would have never been so foolish. To my surprise the queen gave a single nod, a gesture I chose to interpret as assent. When she spoke, she did so without contempt or malice, and maybe even with a hint of sympathy. "You will invoke the Right?" It was a statement more than a question.

"I must," I replied, my voice hardly more than a whisper.

Someone nearby spoke in hushed tones, "The Right."

"He's invoked the Right," someone else said, a little louder.

A low murmur rippled through the crowd.

Page upon page of 'The Free People's Charter', the document codifying the rules by which the humans had lived aboard the Hawking, were devoted to defining what humans called "rights", which mostly consisted of things Atipok granted one another as due course and the natural state of things. As I understood it, such definitions were necessary because of how often humans denied one another such basics. Every group of humans had their own idea about what was or wasn't a right, and they squabbled about it often. Sometimes, they killed one another over it.

In contrast, there was only one thing, one fundamental claim granted of each and every Atipok: the Right of a democratic phee duel.

Phee doesn't pick sides. Phee wielded by the unjust is just as potent as if wielded by the righteous. Our ancestors realized this and, in their wisdom, learned how to lend a community's collective might to an Atipok standing up for what they believe in, to concentrate power to a single individual willing to make a stand. Such channeling was the same, in principle, as when the queen had bolstered my working to heal the nestling's crushed tail in the marketplace. The queen and I would duel, and any Atipok could lend their strength to either combatant.

Of course, in this particular instance, the democratic nature of the duel was a moot point. The queen would need no assistance, nor would anyone offer it. It would be insulting. And no one would back me.

Queen Phallat sighed. "That's a shame," she said quietly. Then, louder, she said, "So be it. Die well, Healer Takey."

"Thank you, pha." I experienced no flare of indignation at the implication that my death was the only possible outcome. It was as true as the egg I'd hatched from.

I looked around, hoping to see some flicker of understanding of why I was doing what I was doing, but saw only angry scowls. I glanced to where Cordek had stood, fully expecting some smug expression of satisfaction at my certain demise, but he was nowhere to be seen.

A cadre of the queen's guards led Molly and me to the Ovidium floor. As the subject of the duel, Molly was required to be present. She stood a dozen paces behind me, her shoulders held by a particularly large guard. The queen squared off twice as far in front of me. Everyone else cleared the floor. As the last of our escort disappeared through the lone entrance, the crowd grew suddenly silent. For a long moment, the Ovidium was still. My scales stood on edge. I felt as if I were passing through a dream, not in control of my actions, like some unseen and particularly cruel puppeteer was pulling my strings.

I bowed deeply, my nose brushing the ice-smooth floor. Queen Phallat gave a short nod and then drew an almost insubstantial barrier of phee cascading back over her head in a semitransparent dome of power. It was a signal, an invitation to make the first attack.

A rapt murmur rippled through the stands.

I hesitated. Why would she go on the defensive? Why not crush me and be done with it? I racked my fear-addled brain for an explanation. All I could come up with was another question: why raise such a thin shield? It was an insult; a slap in the face. Everyone knew I didn't stand a chance. Why rub my face in it?

The weight of the Ovidium's silence pressed around me, my breaths coming short and fast.

"So be it," I growled through clenched teeth. My fingers clawed before me, I gathered phee into a writhing mass of energy. I wouldn't insult my queen with a weak effort. I would honor her with my very best.

I was no warrior. Martial phee never intrigued me like it did so many of my nestmates, but as a healer, I'd traveled more than most. I'd seen pheework firsthand that many have only heard of. I settled on a strategy, coaxing phee up my legs, over my back, down my arms, out, out, out, extending my appendages to monstrous proportions. On the end of my new phee-arms I willed huge razor-tipped claws, my recent chatraka encounter fresh in my mind.

As soon as phee coalesced at the tip of the last claw, I attacked. The crowd gasped as I raked the massive claws over the queen's thin shield, sparks of phee shearing off with a staccato crackle. I didn't wait to see the effect of my attack. I attacked again. Over and over I clawed and gouged at the matriarch of our people. I'd never harnessed so much phee for so long in my life. From every angle I tested her shield. With every ounce of strength, I pushed. The air hummed and shrieked with the power of my attack.

Finally, what seemed like ages later, my knees gave out. My phee-arms drained back into the flow and I collapsed, panting on the pearl floor, my skull pounding as if threatening to implode.

I knew what I would see but even then, when I finally managed to lift my head, part of me was still surprised to see Queen Phallat standing there, unmoved, serene even, as if I'd just finished singing her a tune rather than giving my all to end her life.

The wisdom of her tactic dawned on me. Offering me the first blow had been a generous, even merciful act. Her already adoring subjects would write ballads celebrating their queen's compassion. The queen knew full well that my best attack couldn't so much as scratch her thinnest shield. I had given her my all and failed spectacularly. Without so much as raising a hand she'd demonstrated her power for all to see. And now I was exhausted. Whatever paltry defense I might muster would be only a fraction of what it would have been. Her victory would be quick and decisive. Mercifully so. She had played the game perfectly.

The queen finally moved. With slow deliberate motion, she raised her outstretched arms, her fingers clawing upward as if lifting a great weight. The phee boiled around her, responding with loving enthusiasm to her every whim. I scrambled to my feet, somehow, and watched in awe as she gathered more and more phee, more phee than I'd ever seen a single Atipok wield. Then, with a lunge, she directed the staggering volume of power directly at me in an uninterrupted solid column.

I was a tatim beetle before a tempest, a daisy before a dolk stampede. All I could do was throw up my strongest shield and cower behind it. The column slammed into my barrier, driving me back across the pearl floor. I toppled backward only to see the column pivot, now perpendicular to the floor, to crush me like an old eggshell. The column dropped and my shield slammed against me, pinning me to the ground. I was trapped, unable to press back against the staggering volume of phee. My shield collapsed further until my breaths came short and shallow. My vision blurred as my head threatened to split like an overripe melon.

Then, among the flashes of light flickering at the edges of my dimming consciousness, one suddenly shone brighter: a white flash far, far above. I tried to turn my attention to it but couldn't, my focus stolen by the crushing weight. My time had come. I heard the crowd cheer as the last of my will drained from me. The very ground I laid on, the impossibly smooth pearl that crushed my bones, jumped and rocked as if eager to swallow me up. My shield failed.

And the weight was gone.

I gasped, the darkness giving way to incomprehensible light and sound. The room swayed and pulsed into fuzzy focus, my eyes throbbing in my skull, the crowd's roar having reached a crescendo. I blinked hard, trying to clear my vision, not trusting my eyes, not wanting to understand what I saw before me. But when I opened them again the scene was the same.

There, like a tooth broken from the mouth of the Great Mother herself, where only breaths before Queen Phallat had rained her awful power down upon me, sat the largest of the Ovidium's stalactites, half-embedded in the now cracked pearl floor.

Nothing was left of the queen.

My muddy mind slowly realized that the crowd wasn't cheering. They were crying out in grief, bathing the great hall in an orgy of agony the likes of which would have been unimaginable in any other circumstance. Grief is generally a subdued, private affair among Atipok. But the loss of the greatest of us, our flesh and blood link to the Great Mother, it tore asunder all usual social norms.

I managed to find my own voice.

"No," I spat, the word tinged with blood that spattered the pearl floor. I crawled on my hands and knees, searching the phee that coursed around the embedded spire for some sign of life, but finding none.

I struggled to push through the haze, to understand what had happened. I should be dead. There was never a chance that I would survive the duel. I had accepted that. Had I somehow bested the queen? It couldn't be possible. I should be dead. But I wasn't. Had some freak accident saved me?

I dropped to a hip and looked up to the great domed ceiling, finding the stub of the fallen stalactite. My eyes traced the outer edge of the circular cross-section, the arc clean and even like a cut, not jagged like a break.

I didn't beat the queen, I realized. I couldn't have, wouldn't have desecrated the Ovidium. No Atipok would. Neither would one interfere in the Right.

I pivoted on my hip to look back at the human. Still restrained by her guard, her wide-eyed alien face wasn't turned toward me, or even the entombed queen, but instead craned upward, her eyes on the former home of the stalactite.

A wave of betrayal washed over me. "What have you done?" I screamed over the cacophony.

Her wide eyes met mine.

"What have you done?" I echoed. She flinched and the deema hummed a warning. I didn't care. Before I even consciously recognized the action I was on my feet, staggering toward the human, the outsider, the only one capable of such sacrilege. The deema bit at the base of my skull but I ignored it. With my dying breath, I would find justice for this treachery.

Cordek stopped me.

I didn't even know he was there. One moment I was charging at the girl with vengeful intentions, the next I was again crushed against the smooth pearl floor, a less impressive but still effective column of phee tinged with the commander's essence immobilizing me.

The commander strode from the single entrance, his steps steady and measured, a half-dozen soldiers in his wake. A ball of phee enveloped the girl, each soldier in Cordek's escort adding a layer. The human, for her part, seemed rooted to the floor where she cowered, wrapped in her blanket and paralyzed with fear. Cordek stopped when he reached me, crouching down low until our eyes met. "All traitors must be brought to justice," he said.

I thought his choice of words odd but his tone was even and confident, and part of me felt instantly reassured. The authorities were here. They had the human contained. Whatever my differences with Cordek, he would do what needed to be done to avenge our queen.

Cordek straightened, raising a hand to the crowd. The roar of the great hall faded to a heavy silence. He lowered his hand and walked over to the stalactite, the pillar towering over him despite being half buried in the floor. Head bowed, he rested a hand against its glossy mass before turning to survey the assembled thousands.

"My Atipok." He had drawn a thin bubble of phee over his mouth to amplify his voice so that all could hear. "Our beloved queen is dead," he announced gravely.

Renewed cries of anguish and outrage rippled through the stands. Cordek let it continue for a few long moments before again raising a hand.

The sound died away.

"She has been murdered!" He stretched out his arms, gesturing to the Ovidium. "Here, in this, our most holy place."

The crowd rumbled. Phee churned and writhed through the stands, whipped into a fervor.

"During our most holy season!" Cordek continued.

The rumble deepened, the sound mirroring the anger boiling in my own chest.

"Murdered at the hands of a human, an alien that has somehow perverted the will of the Great Mother, that has somehow corrupted the phee to turn it against us!" He pointed at Molly.

The stands erupted in a collective howl of rage. I was sure the girl didn't understand what was being said. Very few humans speak Atipok and she'd given no indication she could follow my conversation with the queen, but she seemed to understand the focus of the crowd's hostility. She shrank into herself, cowering even further under her blanket.

Cordek allowed the howl to fade before continuing. "Long have I warned of the dangers of opening our lands to the humans. Long have I sought to stop their invasion. They are not of the Great Egg! They don't belong here! Their very presence here is an affront to the Great Mother!"

The crowd rumbled in agreement. Even I, after solars of working with humans, even after calling some of them friends, found myself stirred by his words.

"I knew, in time, the humans would reveal themselves to be treacherous, that the day would come when they would take advantage of our beloved queen's endless generosity and compassion. That they should have attacked her directly though, I had never considered." He paused, as if in reflection. "In hindsight, it seems obvious. Remember how they concentrated their fire on her litter during the Battle of the Red Plain? I wish I had seen it coming. I wish I had known that today would be the day."

He bowed his head.

"What I couldn't know," he said quickly, jerking upright to attention, "what I would have never accepted, is that we would be betrayed from within."

My mind tumbled with the same questions being shouted from the stands. What was he getting at? Had an Atipok had betrayed us? Who would do such a thing?

"Betrayed by an Atipok corrupted by solars of human influence," he continued.

No. He couldn't mean…

Cordek pivoted, sweeping his silk-banded arm across his body until he pointed at me. "Betrayed by one of our very own!"

For the briefest moment I thought to turn my head to see the vile yolk-snatcher behind me. Of course, there wasn't anyone behind me.

The accusation hit me like an electric charge, shorting out my brain. I couldn't process. I couldn't understand. I blinked, unable to react on even an emotional level, let alone a cognitive one. I just lay there, numb, dumb, and unmoving.

Cordek raised his hands again, quieting the crowd's roar I only now noticed. "I'm afraid that's not all. This wasn't the action of two rogue despots. This was a deliberate attack coordinated by the human leadership." He paused, the space around him seeming to shrink as the crowd collectively learned forward to hear his conclusion. "During the Right, while this traitor distracted and the human murdered our late queen, human forces attacked Salitat."

I barely heard the crowd's reaction. My mind had kicked into gear and was too busy racing through the events since Hassan and I found the girl in the rubble of her home. Had it all been a lie? Had the humans staged the whole thing, sacrificed the girl's family in some desperate attempt to murder our queen? It didn't seem possible. Hassan wouldn't do that. Would he?

"They waited until Atalan began, until the traitor had claimed the Right, to launch their attack. If not for the bravery of my soldiers, several of whom gave their lives to defend this city, we might have been overrun."

I wracked my brain. How could the humans have known when the Right began? Or what it even was in the first place? I'd never told Hasan such a thing. Had I?

"What say you, Traitor?"

I started at Cordek's voice in my ear. I hadn't noticed him squat beside me.

"It can't be," is all I managed. It all seemed too much. It just didn't add up.

"He denies it!" Cordek announced to the crowd, standing. "Let us show him!"

The column of phee pinning me down dissolved and two of Cordek's soldiers jerked me to my feet. We were led from the Ovidium floor up one of the long staircases through the stands. Or rather Molly was carried in a ball of multi-colored phee and I was shoved, dragged, and thrown up the Ovidium steps. By the time I was dumped outside into the light of the mid-morning suns, my mouth was bleeding and the lid of my left eye was starting to swell. I squinted my good eye at the angry mob as a soldier hauled me to my feet. My knees buckled but hands on each arm kept me upright. We were paraded through the streets to the plaza just inside the south gate. There, laid on their backs side by side in a crooked row next to a wagon, were the bodies of the human attackers. There were a dozen males and half as many females, all dark skinned, each with a plasma rifle or pistol lying at their feet. The soldiers released me and I fell to my knees.

There was a brilliant flash of white and the girl screamed. "Bobby!"

The soldiers that had been restraining the girl staggered backwards, their phee ball shattered. I blinked away stars to see her crouched atop one of the dead humans, a tall skinny male with short cropped fur. "No," she sobbed over his broken form. "Bobby, no."

One of the soldiers stepped toward her but Cordek waved her off. "You know this human?" the captain asked Molly in surprisingly good human.

"He's my brother," she growled, tears streaming down her face.

Brother? Yes, I could see the resemblance, the girl's softer features echoed in the squarer lines of the older male.

"You see!" Cordek addressed the crowd. "She admits to being nestmates with their leader!"

"He's my brother!" she screamed this time. "What did you dirty lizards do to him?"

I closed my eyes to the poor timing of her words. Most Atipok could claim to know only a short list of human words or phrases. 'Dirty Lizard', the most insulting of a fairly long list of human pejoratives for Atipok, was near the top of every list.

Angry hisses sounded around us.

"There you have it," Cordek announced as if the slur explained everything. He nodded to a soldier who stepped forward to collect the girl. She fought so fiercely that Cordek nodded to another soldier. In the end, it took three to pry her off her dead kinsmen. "The humans have shown their true selves." Cordek stepped onto the wagon, his phee-bubble-amplified voice booming out over the crowd. "And their crimes cannot go unpunished. It's time we do what we should have done the day they arrived."

The crowd rumbled in agreement. Other than a small area around the dead humans, the plaza was packed shoulder to shoulder, front to tail.

"The humans have tried to cut off our head," he told the crowd. "To leave us weakened for their next attack. We cannot allow ourselves to be vulnerable. We will have a new queen, and she will unite us as we must be united. But the confirmation process takes time; time we don't have. The humans would not have made such a bold move unless they planned to act upon it. We cannot let that happen. We must move first. We must strike the next blow. We must stand united until a new queen can be appointed."

The crowd was nothing but rapt attention and nods.

"I never wanted this. I have dedicated my life to bringing peace and order to all Atipok. I have never sought power. But as legion commander, I will shoulder this burden for a time, to do what needs to be done. I will lead. If you'll have me," he added with a small bow.

The crowd erupted, quickly settling into a chant of, "Pha, pha, pha." I scanned the eager faces around me for any sign of dissent but found none.

Cordek stood tall, surveying the masses before quieting them with a gesture. "We will deal with the human problem," he said, hopping off the wagon. He turned to me, still on my knees in the street. "But first, we will take care of our own. If this Atipok has sided with the humans, he will share their fate."

A yolk of phee shoved my shoulders to the ground, pinning me prone in the dusty street. I managed to turn my head just enough to see a sharply-angled cleaver of phee gather to hang poised in the air above my neck. I clenched my eyes shut, shaking as the mob cheered.

All I'd ever done was try to live up to my mother's legacy. Instead, I would die in the street, executed as a traitor.

"Stop!" a phee-amplified voice rose above the din.

A voice I knew.

I opened my eyes to see Dalia step out of the quieted mob, a thin bubble of phee over her mouth. Her eyes met mine for the briefest moment before she turned to Cordek, the bubble slipping away. "You can't kill him."

"What is this? Do you side with him?" Cordek stepped into my line of sight, pointing at me, then at Molly. "Do you side with the humans?"

Phee boiled at Dalia's feet in warning. "Take care in what you say, Commander."

"You dare threaten me?" Now it was Cordek visibly shaking, not with fear but with rage. A collective gasp from the crowd prompted me to look up, the blade above my head now angled at Dalia.

"Not to threaten you," she said, eyeing the blade. "To help you. To help us all. The traitor—"

The phee cleaver couldn't have hurt much more than the stab in my middle when she nodded towards me.

"He's protected. He claimed the Right and defeated the queen."

"Through deception and betrayal!" Cordek fumed.

"You know as well as I do, the Right makes no distinction. Cordek, we are under attack. Now more than ever we must maintain who we are. We must uphold our values. The Right is sacred. It must be honored."

A murmur of agreement sounded from the crowd.

Cordek glanced around before straightening. He took a visibly deep breath. The blade above my neck trickled away, though the yolk remained. "Thank you, Dalia. Your wisdom and council won't be forgotten," he said, an edge to the promise sharper than the cleaver that had nearly ended me.

Dalia gave a small bow and stepped back, her eyes once again meeting mine before fading into the crowd. I had the gut-churning feeling that I might never see those eyes again.

"As for you, Traitor," Cordek turned to me, "you have been granted the opportunity to share the human's fate directly. You are henceforth banished from all things Atipok." The yolk dissipated only to be replaced by two soldiers jerking me to my feet. "No Atipok will harbor nor aid you." He nodded toward the south gate and the soldiers dragged me forward.

I couldn't even muster the will to resist. That is, not until the deema hummed at the base of my skull. I managed to plant my feet enough to make the soldiers pause. "What of the girl?" I called back over my shoulder.

Cordek sneered. "The Right does not protect her. She will stay here to pay for her crimes." He gestured to the soldiers and they resumed dragging toward the gate, although this time I put up as much of a fight as I could manage.

It did no good.

"Run, traitor Takey," Cordek shouted over my efforts. "Run back to the humans you betrayed us for. Run back and share in their extermination!"

The air left my lungs when I hit the ground, the soldiers having tossed me the last few paces out the gate. As the large wooden doors closed behind me, I heard Cordek's call. "Amass the army! Tomorrow, we march on the humans! Tomorrow, we take back our world!"

My people cheered.

All I could do was lay in the dirt, coughing and bleeding, as the massive doors shut behind me with a dull clang.

The roads were empty; all my kin were back at Salitat. I'd been walking for hours and hadn't seen so much as a stray sentry. Even the phee seemed sparse, thin strands stretched across the sandy red plains like a fraying blanket. It was an odd feeling, like I was the only one of my kind in the world. In a way, I was. In my attempt to bridge the divide between Atipok and human, I'd been cut from both sides, left to fall into the abyss.

Slow and steady, I walked the path I'd taken from Shiptown only two days before, more out of a lack of anywhere else to go than a real desire to end up there. What would I say to the humans? To Hassan? They had betrayed me, using the girl, the only human pheeworker, as an assassin. I wondered if her family had readily sacrificed themselves or if they'd been murdered for the cause. At this point, I wouldn't put anything past the humans. I'd worked so hard to help them and in the end, they'd just used me.

And now the queen was dead.

And tomorrow the Atipok army would follow in my footsteps and kill every last human. Despite what they'd done to me, to my people, the thought of their annihilation churned my empty stomach. My own legacy hadn't survived the morning. My mother's wouldn't survive the following day.

I limped along in no real hurry, the twin suns well past their zeniths, my left eye swollen shut, my right side aching. I was pretty sure my tail was broken. Needles of hot pain radiated down its length with every step. As a healer, I could have stopped and bound phee to my wounds, but I didn't see the point. So, I limped on.

There was so much I didn't understand. Why had the humans done this? What did they hope to gain? Did they think that murdering our leader would grant them a military advantage? Did they not understand that they'd ordered their own execution?

Why had Hassan, my friend, betrayed me?

Over and over, I replayed the morning's events in my mind. In the Ovidium, could I have done something to protect the queen? At the south gate, could I have said something to prove my innocence? At the south gate—

I stopped.

The south gate.

I closed my good eye, brow furrowed, trying to picture the scene clearly. The stiffness in the young male's arms as Molly shook her brother's shoulders. The chalky pallor of his skin. The dried blood around his mouth, brown and flaking.

Suddenly I wasn't alone. From a tall thicket of saber bushes not two dozen paces ahead, a young female chatraka bounded onto the wide road. She was gold with faint stippling on her wide beak, a spitting image of the animal I'd seen only days before, save that this one looked decidedly more harried. Dark matted fur marked a wound on her shoulder and a jagged crack traced the curve of her beak. When she stopped, she held one of her hind legs cocked awkwardly, favoring the paw.

The chatraka eyed me, then turned as if to duck back into the saber bushes only to stagger back. She broke for the other side of the road but again stumbled back as if struck by some unseen force.

Or maybe not unseen. I blinked my good eye, not trusting it.

The chatraka turned toward me, eyes darting to either side, searching, as if for an escape route. It bobbed its massive head into the thin flow of phee. With a snort, it suddenly bolted straight for me.

I tensed, waiting to be ripped by talon and beak, but instead the great animal leapt, clearing the space above my head with ease before landing with a pivot to one side, making for a patch of sweetgrass a few wagon lengths off the road.

She'd nearly made it when—

Snap!

The chatraka tumbled back onto her haunches with a shriek, the crack on her beak noticeably wider than before.

Eyes wide, I backed slowly away. I'd finally seen what had forced her back.

White phee.

But then again, not exactly white. Molly's phee was as brilliant as new fallen snow. This phee was the same snow along a road half a lunar later, still white but dirty and dull. The tainted phee badgered and batted at the great hunter, corralling her back onto the road and toward me.

I thought of my recent chatraka encounter and how ineffective my own attack had been. White phee must be as befuddling to the predator as it was to us Atipok. I looked around, desperate to spot the source of the ribbon, but saw no one, human or otherwise.

I held my hands out in front of me. "Easy." It was only a couple dozen paces away. "Easy."

I plucked a single strand of phee without lifting it from the flow. Casting my sight along the strand I watched from the ground as it streamed under the belly of the beast. The chatraka was backing away, creeping off to one side of the road. Aiming for that side, I arced the strand upward. Just as I'd suspected, as soon as she stepped off the road a ribbon of dirty white phee sprang up from the flow to slap her in the haunch, halting her escape.

I lunged, stretching my strand to meet the ribbon before it could sink back into the flow. It dodged, but my single stand was more agile than the thick ribbon.

I juked.

We touched.

And time froze, the moment suspended midair with beautiful, terrible clarity, like one of the giant phee pestles during the Battle of the Red Plain.

The phee was a blend of two workers: human and Atipok. Surprisingly, the human component, the snow, wasn't Molly. But it was the Atipok portion, the grime on the snow, that nearly stopped my heart.

It was Cordek.

I understood. With a lucidity painfully sharp, I understood. The tainted phee, the dead humans at the south gate, the Atipok hatchlings murdered by plasma rifles, the chatraka attacks over the last few lunars.

All of it.

I heaved the strand away from the ribbon, turning it to look back at the chatraka, and past it myself, my body, standing on the road a dozen paces past the chatraka. My pheework seemed to have triggered something in the beast. Perhaps she now associated me with her tormentor. Regardless, she no longer needed prodding. Her goal was clear. Haunches flexed, hind claws digging into the packed soil of the road, she tensed to charge at my unseeing eyes.

I reeled in the strand, returning to my eyes just as the chatraka lunged, cutting the space between us in half with a single bound. I tensed to dive to the side but before I could move, a blow to my midsection knocked the breath from my lungs.

The chatraka skidded to a halt where I'd been standing only a heartbeat before, turning a full circle in obvious confusion.

Gasping, I hung in the air above its head, equally confused, suspended by a band of burnt orange phee wrapped around my torso.

It was Hohonus. I could sense the blustering healer in the band. Regaining my breath, I looked around to see a delicate cord of light blue phee dance into the space the chatraka had occupied heartbeats before. It had to be Landly.

Somehow, the blue cord was able to interact with Cordek's off-white ribbon, looping around it before tugging it toward the chatraka. It must have been the blend of phees. The alien portion allowed Cordek to bully chatraka like no Atipok before him. But the other component, the Atipok portion, could still be manipulated by other Atipok.

The blue cord tugged and pulled the white ribbon around the chatraka, corralling the beast, forcing it slowly off the road toward the patch of sweetgrass and away from me. Landly's strength was impressive. I knew he was a skilled healer, but I was still surprised to see how he bullied Cordek.

Hohonus' band lowered me to the ground and broke away to join the fray.

I grabbed my own rope of phee, coursing over to help, brushing against the blue cord as I went. It was Landly, but not just Landly. Dalia was there too. She must have been channeling for him back in Salitat. All four Atipok were working from the city, Cordek included. Distance pheework like that was difficult but this was a legion commander and three senior healers, amongst the most skilled pheeworkers alive.

The healers had Cordek pretty well contained, blocking his every attempt to reel in his ribbon and escape. The chatraka was a different story. The healers could prevent Cordek from leaving but bullying his white ribbon to shield me was proving difficult. The huge predator juked and ducked, still determined to get to me. They were only just managing to keep it at bay.

I looped my rope around, trying to figure out where I could do the most good, only to have it slapped back by Hohonus' burnt orange band. I moved forward again but was again rebuked. Hohonus' band wrapped around mine, throwing it back toward my body.

It took me a moment, but I got the message. He was telling me to run.

My heart swelled with gratitude. My friends were risking everything for me. They couldn't contain Cordek forever. Eventually he would break free and return to himself. Then he would hunt down my fellow healers with every resource at his disposal. How they'd followed the commander, or how much of his scheme they'd figured out, I couldn't know. But one thing was sure: they believed in me.

I returned to myself. "Thank you," I said, even though it wasn't close to enough.

I turned and ran in the direction I'd been headed all along, only now with desperate purpose. I had to get to Shiptown.

I had to warn Hassan.

It took me longer than I liked to reach Shiptown. I knew Atipok who could use phee to lengthen their legs to extend their gait. Getting the proportions and rhythm right was a real trick and unfortunately, as evidenced by the long scrape on my shoulder, one I'd never mastered. The full moon glowed green in the sky like the always-judging eye of the Great Mother by the time I finally saw the first dimly lit shacks on the outskirts. As before, two soldiers with plasma rifles greeted me. I asked to see Hassan without breaking stride. Thankfully they didn't try to stop me, assuring me he would be found in the town square with everyone else. It made no sense given the hour, but I was in no mood to question. I plodded on, the soldiers falling in beside me as an escort.

It wasn't long before I saw what they'd meant. The heart of Shiptown was a bustle of activity. Brightly colored lanterns dangled from the Hawking and the smell of roasted dolk filled the air. Fires burned in large metal braziers on either side of the stage where a band screeched some awful human attempt at music.

How very like humans to throw a party on the eve of their own extinction.

"Where is he?" I asked the soldiers. By the time one of them spotted Hassan, off to one side of the stage talking with Mahira, quite a few humans had spotted me. A tense murmur spread through the gathering, mixing oddly with the merrymaking. Hassan must have heard the change. He turned as I approached, his features creased with concern. Our eyes met.

I was overwhelmed with a sudden need to apologize to my friend. I had allowed myself to be convinced he'd betrayed me and in doing so, the opposite was true. I had betrayed him. But there wasn't time for that now.

"Takey?" He stepped forward. "What are you doing here? Is Atalan over?"

I stepped close. "You need to call the council."

His brow creased. "What? Why?"

"I'll explain what I can to the council."

He glanced briefly at Mahira who stood by his side with a similarly concerned expression. "Takey, what's going on?" he asked. "Where's Molly?"

From behind me, a familiar voice spoke up before I could. "That's a very good question," Chan said. "Where is Molly?"

Shells, I had hoped to avoid Chan, or at least address the full council where his blustering might be tempered by his peer's relative level-headedness.

I took a deep breath and turned to meet the towering human's hostile gaze. "She's in Salitat."

"Back at lizard city?" His tone mocked me. "But how can that be? You gave a death promise that you would bring her back." He mugged for the crowd. "If she's not here, shouldn't you be dead?"

My deema pounded as if angered by Chan's words. "I said I would save her and as far as I know she's still alive. She's being held—"

"As far as you know? Being held?" The mockery in his voice was gone, replaced by pure malice. He closed the distance with a step and thrust a finger into my chest. "Are you telling me the little girl we entrusted to your care has been kidnapped? That she might be dead?" He punctuated his question with a stab of his finger.

I struggled to stay calm. I could defend myself if it came to it and Chan wouldn't stand a chance. But he was still big and ugly and right in my face; phee or no, he was intimidating. "There was an incident," I said evenly. "She's been accused of a crime."

"What kind of incident?" Hassan asked behind me.

Other than a brief stop to bind my injuries, my whole trek to Shiptown had been consumed with the question of how much to tell the humans. They needed to know that an army was coming to destroy them if they had any chance to survive. But the rest of it? Those were Atipok matters. I had no desire to point out the cracks in our collective egg.

I took a deep breath. "As I said, as far as I know she's safe. That means my deema, my life oath, still holds."

Chan snorted and the crowd rumbled.

I pressed on. "And that I will go back to Salitat and give her what aid I can. But there are more pressing matters."

Mahira stepped forward. "Healer Takey, what could possibly be more important than the fate of one of our children?"

Before I could answer the crowd behind us grumbled and parted to allow an out-of-breath young male with red cheeks. "Sir," he panted to Chan. "The Atipok. They're gathering outside their city. All of them. It looks like an army."

A nervous murmur rippled through the crowd as every eye turned to me, Hassan's and Chan's included.

"That's what I was about to tell you," I said quickly. "That's why I'm here. I came to warn you."

"Or to distract us," Chan growled.

I ignored him. "The army will march on Shiptown at first light. They mean to wipe you out."

Everyone spoke at once but it was Mahira's voice I heard. "But why?"

I shook my head. "There isn't time to explain. You must leave. Now. Gather what you can and go."

Hassan spread his hands. "Go where?"

"You once told me that you saw land on the other side of this world, from your ship, across the Green Sea." I pointed to the east. "You must go there. Now."

Cries of protest this time. But it was Chan's voice that carried. "This is a ploy! They mean to scare us from our homes." He pointed at the spaceship. "They want the Hawking. They want our technology. They're tired of living in caves."

I wheeled on him. "I thought you said we lived in stone mansions and you lived in shacks. Why would we want to trade?" Phee bubbled at my feet, responding to my frustration.

A hand on my arm turned me. It was Hassan. "Takey, even if we wanted to, we don't have the means to move all these people to the coast, let alone across the sea."

"If you stay, none will survive. If you go, many will be lost, but you won't lose all." I couldn't know that for sure. The Green Sea was treacherous. Even Atipok who had sailed those waters for generations seldom strayed out of sight of land. And those that did seldom returned.

"Enough lies!" Chan shouted to the crowd. "We were fools to let him take the girl to lizard city. Lord knows what they did to her. No doubt they tortured her for information for this attack. I am certain she's dead. And now he's trying to scare us from our homes without a fight! Are we to be made fools again?"

The accusations were ludicrous. Anyone that took a moment to think would realize that a nestling from an outlying settlement was hardly a source of intelligence. But the faces around me didn't reflect thoughtful consideration. They betrayed only fear and anger. Even Hassan and Mahira looked doubtful.

"We must defend ourselves." Chan raised a fist. "We must fight!"

The crowd cheered.

Chan was head of the human militia, a fact he brought up often and a role he now stepped into. "Go now! Round up every able-bodied man, woman, and child. Gather every weapon you can get your hands on. Report to your section commanders."

"This is foolish," I growled.

"And you," Chan pointed at me but looked around the crowd. "Seize the lizard," he ordered a thick-set male.

"Don't." I didn't raise my voice, and he couldn't see the phee boiling at my feet, but the man hesitated.

Chan didn't. "I said seize him!"

The man advanced.

I let him take two steps before I swept his legs out from under him. His back hit the packed red dirt of the square with a thud and he let out a huff of expelled air.

The square was suddenly silent. "Don't," I repeated. "Don't even try it."

"Or what?" Chan chided. "You'll destroy us with your black magic?" He gestured to the man. "Get up. He's bluffing."

"I could destroy you." My stomach clenched at my own words. They didn't sound like words I would say, but they kept coming. "I could kill every last one of you. By myself. It would take a while but I could do it. You couldn't stop me."

The man, who had gotten to his feet, took a wary step back, fear in his eyes. I hated that fear and hated myself for causing it. But I'd been pushed too far.

"But you won't." It was Hassan.

I kept my eyes on Chan. "Why not?"

"Because it's not what's best for Molly," he said.

I hesitated. It seemed an odd reply. Then I realized it only made sense if Hassan believed Molly was alive and the deema intact, and that I was still doing everything I could to help her. It meant he still believed me.

"You're right." I straightened, my shoulders relaxing. "I won't harm you."

The man took a step forward.

"But neither will I allow you to hold me."

"So now what?" Chan barked. "Do you expect us to let you walk out of here? So you can, what? Report back to the lizard army?"

I suppressed a mirthless chuckle at what that army would do to me. Chan would love that.

Hassan answered before I could. "I take full responsibility for Takey. He'll be under my watch and my protection."

"No good," someone shouted from the remains of the crowd, no longer content to let their leaders handle things. "He's the one what talked us into letting that girl go. He's practically one of them."

There were shouts of anger from a couple men I recognized as Hassan's people followed by sounds of a scuffle.

"Enough," Chan boomed. "The lizard will stay with Hassan. The rest of you, do as I've ordered. Report to your commanders."

Hassan grabbed my arm and started to lead me from the square.

Chan stepped in front of us. "Where do you think you're going?"

"To my post," Hassan said. "I'm a regional commander. You know that."

"Not today you're not. Not with him. You will stay here," he pointed at the ground, "in the square, and guard the prisoner."

Hassan started to protest.

"That's an order." Chan leaned so close to Hassan, the larger man's chin nearly touched Hassan's forehead. Chan's tone dared Hassan to defy him.

For a moment, I thought my friend might. But then he stepped back. "Understood."

Chan gave a nod and turned, striding out of the square with his men.

"Go," Hassan told his people. "Report to your commanders."

They did, leaving us the only two standing in the square, the other humans amassing at the edge of the settlement.

"The Atipok army is coming," I told him. "They will wipe you out. All of you."

He growled, his fists clenched at his sides. "What would you have me do?"

"Take your family and go."

"I can't."

"You can."

"I won't!" he barked. His next words were quiet, but resolved. "I won't abandon my people."

I eyed the stubbornly loyal human, unsurprised. In his skin, I doubted I would do any different. "I understand."

He nodded and looked away. There was shouting all around us, but the square was oddly still, the brightly colored lamps casting a perversely cheery glow on the dark omens of the night. In a patch of blue light to one side of the stage, I saw someone watching us.

Chan's son, Mau, motioned for me to come over.

"Where are you going?" Hassan asked.

I nodded toward the boy and we walked over together.

"Mau, you should have already reported to your father," Hassan said when we reached him.

"I know." The boy looked around, obviously nervous. "But I need to speak with Healer Takey."

"Are you hurt?" I asked.

"No."

"Then what—"

"I just really need to speak to you. Alone."

I glanced at Hassan. "Could you step away for a moment? Just a few paces," I added when he started to protest. "We won't leave the square."

"Fine." He retreated a half dozen steps to stand with his arms crossed.

"Now." I turned back to Mau. "What is it?"

Wringing his hands, he leaned in close, his voice low. "I really need to show you something."

Mau was of an age that he was likely going through the hormonal imbalances humans called puberty. It wasn't unusual for humans of that age to ask me questions they didn't feel comfortable asking their parents. As a member of a different species, it was a dynamic I always found exceedingly odd. "I'm a healer, Mau. You know you can show me anything. Do you need a screen to undress?"

He shook his head. "No. It's not part of me. Not really."

"Okay. Well, I can't leave the square. Can you bring whatever it is to me?"

He clucked a single nervous chuckle. "Oh, it's here already."

I sighed. "Mau, I'm starting to lose patience."

He swallowed, looking around again before meeting my eye. "Okay." He held his hands out from his sides, his palms turned up. Without breaking eye contact he curled his hands up to his shoulders, his fingers clawing the air. From the rainbow flow at my feet, two bands of brilliant white phee coalesced and rose up to wrap around Mau's forearms like Atipok battle silks.

My scales rippled but I managed to keep my voice relatively calm. "You're a pheeworker."

He shrugged. "I guess."

"Have you been able to do this for long?"

"A couple lunars."

"And can you only manipulate white phee?"

He nodded.

"Okay." My mind was oddly blank, like it couldn't handle the implications of what I had just seen. I stared at the white bands.

"There's more," he said.

I felt my good eye twitch. "More?"

He nodded. "There are others."

"Others?" My voice cracked.

"Other whats?" Hassan asked from over my shoulder.

This time we both flinched. I turned to my friend, holding up a finger. "One moment." I turned back to Mau. "How many others?"

"Five, that I know of. Well, six with me."

"Six," I repeated. "Six." I thought of the hours of effort we healers had put into cracking Molly's shield. Three experienced pheeworkers completely stifled. A handful of novices wielding alien phee wouldn't halt the might of the Atipok army, but maybe they could give it pause. "Or at least slow them down a little," I mumbled.

"Six what? Slow who down a little?" Hassan asked.

I ignored him, looking around the square. "Are they here?"

Mau shook his head. "We were planning to use the distraction of the festival to practice. Everyone's in Brett's shed. Or at least, they were," he added.

"Take me to them," I said.

Behind me, Hassan cleared his throat.

I turned and met his eye. "Mau and his friends are pheeworkers." His eyes widened but I pressed on before he could react further. "Their help could be what we need to prevent the extinction of your species. I know you have your orders but do you really want to stop us?"

The human scratched his chin fur for a moment. "No, I suppose I don't."

"Good. Then come with us." I turned back to Mau. "Take us to your friends."

The boy nodded and led us into the torch-lit maze of adobe shacks that was Shiptown.

"It's not like I could've stopped you anyway," Hassan grumbled over my shoulder.

A weaving and winding few minutes later we stopped outside of a relatively large storage shed. I was surprised to see a barrier of semi-transparent white phee covering the door. Mau glanced at me and then extended a ribbon of his own to caress the barrier. It was just the sort of setup an Atipok would use, the touch of phee conveying the identity of the worker on the other side: a phee-password of sorts.

I was impressed.

The barrier dropped and Mau opened the door, ushering us in with impatient gestures. The interior was just as dim as the night outside but instead of flickering torchlight, the space was lit by the slightly blueish glow of a small solar lamp. As Mau had said, five adolescent humans, four females and one male, huddled around the glow in various poses. Mau shut the door and stepped around us to take his place amongst his peers. The shed settled into a tense silence.

I looked around at the shelves lining the walls. Most items I recognized as farming implements: hoes, rakes, and large cloth bags I guessed contained seed. One out of place item caught my eye. Hanging on a peg not far from my head was one of the spherical spacesuit helmets I'd seen used as lampshades. Its curved visor seemed to be looking at me, a crack down its center dividing it into two eyes.

Hassan nudged me and I realized I would need to make the first move. I swallowed. "Thank you for seeing me," I said with a small bow to the group, attempting to convey the respect the meeting deserved.

The greeting was met with furtive glances and silence. One of the females shot Mau a look, tilting her head toward me. Mau cleared his throat. "Thank you for coming, Healer Takey," he said with his own, slightly more awkward bow. "This is Tye, Adamma, Josh, Jenya, and Lucia," he said as he gestured to each of his peers in turn. I recognized Tye, with her angular eyes and long black head fur. I had attempted to treat her mother for a nasty fever only a few lunars before. Unfortunately, the woman had succumbed to seizures and died in my arms. I remembered the stoic way the girl had taken the loss. I also recognized Josh, having set his broken leg two solars back. That bright red fur was hard to forget. The rest I recognized vaguely as residents of Shiptown but hadn't actually met.

"Hello," I said. "I'm sure you all know Hassan."

Nods all around.

The girl Mau had introduced as Jenya stood up. "As-salāmu 'alaykum, Uncle."

At first Hassan didn't react. He just looked at the girl, his face neutral. Finally, he nodded, as if having made a decision. "Wa 'alaykumu s-salām," he said with a small smile.

I turned to Mau, since he seemed willing to speak for the group. "Good. Now that we've got introductions out of the way, I'm afraid our time is short. Is this all of you?"

"That we know of," he said.

"You're all pheeworkers?"

"Some of us are better than others," Lucia offered, drawing chuckles.

"And you've all found this talent recently."

More nods.

"How did you find each other?"

"We just found each other's threads," Josh said with a shrug. "Just wandering around."

They were the only pheeworkers for miles. It would be hard not to cross paths. "But why come to me? Why not tell your parents?"

"Or uncles," Hassan added, his eyes on Jenya.

It was Adamma who spoke up. Her dark skin and braided fur reminded me of Molly and my deema throbbed. "Our families wouldn't understand," she said. "My mom is scared of magic."

"And you know how my father feels," Mau said, his eyes downcast.

"But why me?" I pushed. "Why come to me at all? Why now?"

There was a long pause. "Well, the lizard army is coming, isn't it?" Tye asked in a small voice.

Mau shot her a look. "Atipok," he growled under his breath. "Not lizard."

"Oh." Tye paled. "Sorry."

I ignored the slur. "Yes, my people march on Shiptown," I confirmed. "They'll be here by morning."

"Well," she said again, looking around at her compatriots, "we want to help."

I regarded each member of the circle in turn. They were young and inexperienced, barely more than nestlings, but each met my gaze with firm determination.

My eyes strayed from the circle and again stopped on the helmet, its spherical, bubble-like shape, its cracked visor. The start of an idea tickled the back of my brain. Maybe there was a way. And maybe we could do more than just slow the Atipok army down.

"If I let you help, are you all willing to do as I say?" I asked, my eyes never leaving the helmet.

A pause.

"Yes," Mau said.

I turned to Hassan.

He nodded.

I stepped into the center of the circle, picking up the lamp. "Okay, we've got a lot to cover in very little time. Let's get started."

For only the second time since my hatching, the full might of the Atipok army marched. Like last time, every available pheeworker had dawned the red silks of war. Like last time, their goal was an alien army huddled around the remains of their spaceship. Like last time, fear clutched at my stomach and weakened my knees.

But unlike last time, I now stood on the other side, watching the army approach from beneath a hooded cloak, just one more human waiting to meet his fate to anyone who didn't know better. Hassan stood beside me near the front, hat pulled low, collar up to hide his beard. I wondered if the soles of his feet tickled with the vibration of the footfalls of the approaching thousands as mine did, or if human footwear prevented such sensitivity.

Keeping my hood low, I stole furtive glances at the humans around me. There was fear there. I saw it in the white knuckles gripping weapons, in the tremor stealing up the long barrels of plasma rifles. But there were also set jaws, steel eyes, and small acts of support, like patted backs and nods of encouragement. The humans were resolute. Even facing their destruction, the potential extinction of their species, they stood together.

Foolish or not, it was hard not to admire.

The vibrations stilled as the Atipok army ground to a halt, their front parallel to the humans only a hundred paces away. I recognized the marching formations, the five squadrons of the red army. But instead of the queen's crimson litter leading the center squad, a huge red wagon pulled by a team of six dolk took point. It was at least four times the size of my old wagon, with a closed top rather than an open back. And perched atop, standing behind a deep umber pulpit secured behind the driver, Cordek looked down upon the battlefield.

My deema throbbed with my suspicion of the wagon's contents and my hands shook with contained rage. Cordek had no right to stand in the queen's place at the head of our army. I would prove it, or die trying.

Hassan caught my eye from under his cap and I nodded. The time to act was now, before things got out of hand. Or at least before they got any more out of hand than the brink of war.

For just a moment, I hesitated. Looking into the round brown eyes of my friend, I was hit with a sudden wave of emotion. I wanted to tell Hassan how much it meant to me, his trust, his willingness to stand with me. He must have understood something of what I felt. The human reached out and gave my shoulder a squeeze. One deep breath later, I was pushing my way through the human front.

Shouts sounded from behind me as I stepped into the killing zone between the two armies. I drew a curtain of phee up to protect my back, unsure whether Chan would order his troops to fire on me for interfering, or even do it himself. I still had my hood up, but the cloak only did so much to hide my tail. There was little doubt both sides knew exactly who I was. I angled to put myself directly in front of Cordek's wagon. When I reached the halfway point I dispelled any doubts of my identity, casting aside the cloak and hood with a single motion.

It was the signal my soldiers had been waiting for.

A commotion sounded from the humans to my right. I looked over my shoulder to see Josh, all gangly limbs and red fur, break away from an upset female with a similar red mane, presumably his mother. He stopped a dozen paces ahead of the human front, then nodded my direction, his eyes wide.

Some distance to my left, two more figures stepped out of the crowd: Tye and an older male I recognized as her father. They stopped at around the same distance from the front as Josh. The man bent and kissed Tye on the brow before walking back. She must have told him our plan, or some portion of it. Tye set her feet and gave her own nod.

All along the front my soldiers broke away from their families to stand apart and face the Atipok army. Behind me, Mau was the last to enter the killing zone. He stepped away from his father's side so quietly that Chan, who was busy yelling at Josh to get back in line, didn't notice.

With Mau's nod I took a final deep breath, bracing myself. We'd tested what we were about to try at a much smaller scale back in the shed. It had left my ears ringing.

I raised my hand.

Behind me, my soldiers gathered the bubbling phee flowing toward us along the plain and arched it toward me, bathing me in semitransparent white power. My knees nearly buckled, due to both the sheer power of channeling six pheeworkers and the alien nature of the human pheework. It was unlike anything I'd ever wielded. Much like the humans themselves, it was wilder, less disciplined, harder to control. It was all I could do to keep my feet. But it was still phee, the same ever-present power that had greeted me upon my hatching, had been the tool of my trade, that bound me and my people to the Great Mother.

Slowly, far slower than I would have liked given the uncertainty of Cordek's reaction, I harnessed each flow, merging it into my own, the breadth and depth of my own control expanding past anything I'd ever known. As soon as I'd integrated the last, I released the combined flow, arching up a shield that encased me, my soldiers, and the entire human front. Rather than dirty white, like Cordek's, our combined phee was mother of pearl, a kaleidoscope of shimmering iridescent colors flitting across a cream backdrop.

It was beautiful.

A murmur of uncertainty rippled across the Atipok front. Every one of them had experienced Molly's clumsy bolt of white during the opening moments of Atalan. They knew the power of its alien touch. But Cordek had lied to them. He'd told them that Molly was an anomaly, the only one of her kind. They'd marched on the humans expecting a quick, decisive victory. Our shield was giving them second thoughts.

Good.

I trained my eyes on Cordek. Atop his massive wagon he seemed perfectly at ease. He raised a hand and the murmur quieted, a tense silence settling over the plain.

Of course, Chan chose that moment to spot Mau. His bellow broke the silence. "Mau! What are you doing? Get back in rank!"

The boy didn't react. He stood erect, hands extended in front of him, eyes locked on me as he concentrated on directing phee into our bond.

His father charged into the killing zone. "I said get back in rank!" He reached Mau just after Hassan, who put himself between the bigger man and his son.

"Out of my way!" Chan attempted to shoulder Hassan aside.

Hassan held his ground. "No! Mau is a pheeworker. He and his friends are the only chance we have."

Chan staggered back as if from a blow. "That's a lie."

"No, father." Mau spoke through gritted teeth, his eyes never leaving me. "You can't see it, but we've raised a shield to protect everyone. We're trying to help."

Chan drew his pistol, leveling it at Hassan. "We don't have time for this nonsense. Out of my way."

Hassan raised his hands. "Chan, I know you don't trust me, but trust your son. He's trying to do the right thing."

"My son knows the right thing is to stand with his people!" Chan thrust the weapon closer to Hassan's chest. "Now step aside."

Through our channel, I could feel Mau's conflict: his earnest belief that he was doing all he could to help versus a son's desire to please his father. The bond severed as Mau pulled away. I risked a glance over my shoulder and saw Mau raise his own shield between Chan and Hassan.

"I won't let you shoot him," Mau said, finally turning to face his father.

Chan glared at Mau but addressed Hassan. "I take no pleasure in doing this." The pistol discharged and Hassan staggered back, grasping at his chest. Someone on the human side screamed. Maybe Mahira.

The bolt never made it. The red-hot plasma melted into the barrier and drained away. Hassan patted at his torso, obviously surprised to find it unscathed.

Chan turned the pistol in his hand, looking it over before squeezing off another two shots. Hassan managed a less dramatic reaction this time, only flinching as the bolts dissolved harmlessly into the phee.

"I told you, I won't let you shoot him," Mau said.

Chan looked to me. "What have you done to my son?"

Mau spoke up before I could answer. "No, Dad, this is who I am." He gestured at the other human pheeworkers. "Who we all are. More and more of us will be able to use this power. It will protect us. It will—"

The Atipok attack hit our shield with the force of a battering ram. Stones carried by the phee-driven tempest chipped and shattered in a deafening roar as friction from swirling sands arced electricity across the face of the barrier. The force of it drove me backward, my feet digging furrows through the sand. I flexed my hind claws and braced my tail, needles of pain forcing out a cry as scales sheared off. The shield frayed at the edges like an old rug as I struggled to retain control. Fearful humans cried out behind me, adding to my own roar of pain.

Just as suddenly as it had begun, the attack ended.

I staggered but managed to keep my feet. To my right, Chan had dropped his pistol, his eyes wide and face pale.

"Do you see?" Mau pointed at the shield his father couldn't see. "You would be dead now if it wasn't for us!"

Chan looked to me, then to Hassan, and finally to his son. He opened his mouth to speak, then closed it. Finally, he bowed his head. "Tell me what to do," he said in a small voice.

The humans looked to me. I mentally sorted through our options. The attack had only been a probing shot. Cordek had noticed our distraction and risked a test of our capabilities. Fortunately, the tempest had only been the volley of a single battalion. Unfortunately, it had almost broken us. It confirmed what I'd suspected: even supported by the six humans, well, five since Mau broke off, we couldn't hold off the Atipok army. Not long enough to make a difference.

"Stand with your people," I told Chan. "Give them your strength. Hold them together." I turned to Hassan. "You too. Go to your family. We'll do the rest."

Chan gave his son a quick nod and the two males returned to the front.

I waved my troops in close. "Josh." I nodded to the lanky redhead, letting our channel drop away. "You're up."

The boy paled even further and for a moment I thought he might faint. With a shaky breath, he stepped to one side of our group. Setting his feet, he licked his lips and extended his arms out to either side. Phee boiled and churned around his feet, coalescing from its usual spectrum into a brilliant white mass that flowed up his legs and hips, over his back and shoulders, and down his chest and arms, coating him in a thick armor of liquid power. Phee grasped his legs, lifting him up to tower over his brethren who gasped and backed away. The youth flicked his wrists and white phee shot from his hands, forming pointed lances as long as he was tall. He raked one of the lances along the ground, carving a line in the sand, his eyes trained on Cordek's wagon. Then he stepped back toward the edge of the crowd, his arms and the lances spread protectively in front of his kind.

The humans nearest him scrambled back, gesturing excitedly at the space between him and the ground.

I turned and nodded to Lucia, allowing our channel to melt away.

She nodded back and took position on the opposite side of our group. She touched her fingers to her torso and forehead in a gesture I'd come to associate with one of the human religions, before gathering her own flow of phee. The white power swirled around her feet, coalescing into a churning vortex of sand that lifted her into the air, her long glossy black fur swirling up to stand on end. The humans behind her backed away but this time, and amongst the faces etched with fear there were those filled with awe. The vortex morphed and widened, forming a wall of sand and grit in front of her people, a protective barrier of phee-driven tempest.

I knew the humans couldn't see the cause of the storm or the boy's levitation, but this show wasn't for them. With my second and third best pheeworkers in place, I severed my bonds with the other humans and lowered our shield.

It was a bold move, so bold as to border on foolish. We were unprotected. With a nod, Cordek could unleash an onslaught that would decimate the human forces in a matter of moments. We couldn't stop him and every Atipok present knew it. Dropping our shield amounted to a taunt. A slap in the face daring a response. And if exposing ourselves was a slap, Josh and Lucia's show was a human gesture Hassan had showed me involving brandishing one's middle finger. I was playing on Cordek's arrogance, gambling that he would take our actions as a personal affront. A smart commander would swallow his pride, signal his troops, and we would all die. I was gambling with our lives, not to mention the entire human race, that Cordek wouldn't let the personal challenge, the insult, go unanswered.

The plain hovered in pregnant silence, even the humans sensing the knife-edge position of the moment. I glared at Cordek, pouring every ounce of defiance I could muster into my gaze as if my countenance might be the final peck that broke Cordek's shell.

"Takey," Mau said under his breath. "They're not buying it. We should link back up."

"It's this or nothing." My eyes never left Cordek. "Start gathering phee, all of you."

A high-pitched screech of metal-on-metal broke the silence, followed by a rattling rumble as the giant red wagon slowly ground forward.

We'd done it. Cordek had taken the bait. Even as I watched, the wagon's driver hopped down and scurried back to the Atipok front, assuring that Cordek would face us alone. Cordek stayed perched behind his pulpit, driving the team from on high.

Now came the hard part.

Jenya, Mau, Tye, and my best worker, Adamma, huddled close behind me with Josh and Lucia to either side, maintaining their workings. It didn't take long for the wagon to close the distance, angry phee churning around its massive wheels. As it drew up, I saw two things that surprised me. The first was the pulpit. As Cordek drew closer I saw that it was an exquisitely carved chatraka, its wooden fur so fine as to almost ripple in the breeze. But it wasn't the realism that caught my eye, it was the jagged crack tracing the curve of the chatraka's stippled beak.

The second thing that gave me pause was Cordek's team. Six dolk strong, five of the animals were the finest I'd ever seen: big and powerful with shiny black coats and bright eyes. The sixth, though, was a dusty, old, yellow fleabag half the size and three times the age of the others. My Aesop. There was only one reason to include such a slow, ornery beast at the head of the army. It was a message to me. It was Cordek saying that eventually, everyone bowed to his will.

The wagon stilled. From behind the carved visage of the familiar chatraka, Cordek surveyed my soldiers with his lip curled in a sneer of disgust. "So, you found a few more human abominations?" he said in Atipok.

"Actually, they came to me." I pointed to the sky and the unoccupied members of my troop, who had been waiting for the signal, arched the phee they'd been gathering over the top of our little gathering, encasing the wagon, Cordek, the humans, and me in a dome of white. "I suspect willing channeling is much stronger than coerced."

Cordek glanced up at the dome in mild amusement. "An interesting theory. But even if it's true, what is it you hope to accomplish? Are you and your abominations going to kill me?" He chuckled as if the idea was absurd. "Then what? The entire Atipok force is gathered paces away. Killing me will cement their resolve. You will die and the humans will fall."

He was right. Beyond a shadow of a doubt. He knew it and I knew it. But I couldn't let him know that I knew it. "I will defeat you." I gathered phee, trying to portray a confidence I didn't feel. "I will show our people your weakness and they will see the weakness of your ideas."

The humor drained from Cordek's face. He lifted his hands and phee boiled up the sides of the wagon, seeping into the slots carved near the wheels before emerging from slots near the roof, now augmented and stained a dirty white. "I will let your pet humans live long enough to see you die, then I will use them to clean the stain of their kind from the Great Egg."

"Go for the wagon!" I shouted, launching a tethered javelin of phee at Cordek's head.

Josh broke for the wagon, the spiked boots of his phee armor gouging furrows into the sand. Lucia's sandstorm enveloped him, wiping away the scars in the soil as quickly as they appeared. Cordek parried my javelin with an off-white lance and then batted at Josh with the backswing. Partially obscured by the sandstorm, Josh managed to sidestep the attack, closing on the wagon with his lance raised to strike. I arched another javelin at Cordek, trying to draw his attention back to me. Wrenching two massive boluses of dirty phee up through the wagon, Cordek blocked my missile with one and plowed through the sandstorm with the other. This time there was nowhere for Josh to dodge. The bolus wrapped around him like a hungry eel and chucked him through the air at Lucia. The collision knocked both back against the shield where they dropped unmoving to the ground, their workings trickling away.

I had hoped Josh and Lucia could reach the wagon. Now we were down to the much riskier option. "Mau! Now!" I shouted.

Mau's phee broke from the dome in a thin blade, slicing lengthwise down the center of the wagon. Cordek dove from his pulpit, hitting the ground in a roll that brought him nimbly to his feet. For a moment, the huge red box just sat there. Then, with a wooden creak, the wagon and the wooden chatraka split in two. Dust billowed, then cleared to reveal a tangle of unconscious humans spilled from the bunks lining the walls of the wagon.

I scanned the bodies and breathed a quick sigh of relief. Mau's blade had spared the sleepers. All seven humans appeared whole and, judging by the color of the phee swirling around them, alive.

I couldn't take the time to see the reaction, but I imagined anger rippling across the Atipok front. Coercing another's pheework was the most heinous crime known. It was a perversion of everything Atipok. Cordek's theft of the helpless humans' pheework was indefensible.

My heart skipped as I recognized one of the prone forms, a dark-skinned girl with curly black hair. Rather than a painful pounding, my deema tickled at the sight of her. I knew I was doing everything in my power to help her, and her people.

"You fool!" Cordek shrieked, his phee forking to either side of my defenses to slam me to the ground, the impact driving the air from my lungs. "This was your plan?" He gestured at the now exposed unconscious bodies. "No one will care. You've shown them why I had to use humans to deal with humans. I had to take their alien phee. You've made my case for me!"

I hadn't thought of that.

Mau pivoted his blade and drove it at Cordek from behind.

But the commander was still siphoning phee through the unconscious humans. With a growl he unleashed a wave of power that shattered the youth's blade. Mau tried to run but the wave overtook him, bowling him over, scraping him across the ground, then grinding him up the side of the dome. Suddenly the wave dissolved. Mau fell, hitting the ground with a sickening crack.

Still pinned on my back, I struggled to turn my head. My remaining troops huddled against the wall of the dome, their phee pouring into the shield. I caught Adamma's eye and gave a slight nod, which she returned. The dome constricted.

"Is that it?" Cordek crowed. He stalked to my side to leer over me. With a flick of his hand he lifted me a tail's length into the air only to slam me down into the dusty plain like a child with a doll.

I cried out, the base of my tail radiating pain.

Cordek towered over me again. "It's over, Takey."

Pinned on my back, I could see the peak of the dome, now within a tail's length of Cordek's head. As I watched, the peak parted to reveal a sliver of iridescence shimmering in the morning sunlight. Adamma had pulled it off. It was now or never.

"It's not over!" I growled. "Our people aren't stupid. They'll figure it out! You used chatraka to destroy those human villages! That's where you got your bodies for the fake attack on Salitat! That's where you got the plasma rifles to kill those families outside of Canant! There were hatchlings with them, for Mother's sake!"

Cordek's expression never faltered. "Necessary sacrifices."

"And the queen? Was she a necessary sacrifice? You betrayed her!"

"She'd betrayed us!" Cordek's phee squeezed the breath from my lungs. "She sat by while these eggless humans took over our world. She was the traitor. And like I told you before, all traitors must be brought to justice."

My vision was blurring from lack of air but I managed to slap the ground with my hand. It wasn't the signal we'd agreed on but thankfully my troops figured it out. Tye and Jenya's bisected shield dropped away leaving Adamma's amplification bubble, the latter of which had just broadcast every word of Cordek's confession for every Atipok to hear.

Cordek's expression shifted from triumph to confusion to horror. "What have you done?" he shrieked, bearing down on me even harder.

I didn't have the breath to answer, which was fine since Cordek didn't wait for one. With a growl he whipped his phee skyward, sending me sailing into the air.

As I tumbled high above the plain, my lungs too empty to scream, I briefly wondered if anything we'd done would make a difference. Perhaps it was too late. Perhaps there was just too much fear and anger, on both sides. War might be unavoidable. I wanted to believe it wasn't, but up in the air, unable to reach the phee coursing far below, unable to cushion my fall, I'd never know.

Or at least I wouldn't have known if my friends weren't so quick to react.

I felt Dalia's comforting presence as a gentle cushion of phee caught me mid-air, giving me a perfect vantage point to watch the final scenes of the battle. Cordek had turned his rage on the human front. Adamma and the other conscious humans had managed to raise a shield to protect their kin but were only just holding back the commander's fevered attacks. So frenzied was the latter that he didn't see the rainbow tsunami of power barreling across the plain from the Atipok front until it was too late. He barely had time to flinch before the combined force of all four battalions enveloped him.

Even from my elevated vantage point I could hear his muffled screams break through the jagged gaps carved by bursts of dirty white phee. "No! They are not of the Great Mother! They don't belong here!" Phee bubbled and splashed as he lashed out but despite his desperate flailing, the rainbow began pulling him away, back to the Atipok front. "No! They will overwhelm us! They'll sap our resources! They'll undermine our way of life! We must stop them!" The last tendrils of Cordek's coerced bonds with his former captives severed and the screams grew faint as he was completely enveloped behind the Atipok line.

There was a tingling snap behind my eyes followed by a feeling of profound relief, like a long awaited, full body sneeze. Warmth trickled from the base of my skull down my spine. The deema was gone. I had saved the girl and brought her back to her people. I was free.

Once again, the plain settled into deathly stillness, a brittle silence filling the space between the two armies. My deema may have dissolved, but the threat of war hadn't.

Dalia lowered me to the ground, setting me back in the kill zone near Mau, his father kneeling over him. I collapsed as soon as my feet hit the ground, fatigue washing over me. I managed to crawl over to the humans.

"He's alive." Chan's eyes never left his son's chest. "But his breathing is ragged."

I heard the grind of boots on gravel as Hassan jogged up. "Healer Takey." He squatted beside me. "What's happened?"

I surveyed the Atipok front, still as rigid as ever, still churning with anger and fear.

"Have your people stand down," I told Hassan, my voice not more than a whisper. "Have them drop their weapons."

Hassan looked to Chan, who looked to me pleadingly. "We'll be defenseless."

"You already are."

Chan hesitated.

"Shells, man," I growled. "Just this once, trust me!"

He hesitated a moment, then nodded quickly. "I do." He motioned to Hassan who jogged back to the human front. Moments later, rifles clattered to the ground. I turned to see a series of phee flags pulse up from the Atipok front. It was the signal for retreat. The Atipok army broke and turned for Salitat, taking the encased Cordek with them.

A cheer arose from the human side. I barely noticed. I was on my knees next to Chan, Mau's head in my hands. A quick examination showed two broken vertebrae and a bruised kidney. But it was his lungs that were the issue. The impact had ruptured many of their tiny air sacs and they were filling with fluid. Mau was drowning. I turned to Chan, my vision swimming with exhaustion. "I don't think I can save him."

"I think you can," a familiar voice said from behind me.

I looked up to see Dalia, flanked by Hohonus and Landly.

"So do we," the latter said.

"You bet your sweet tail," Hohonus added.

"Us too." It was Jenya, surrounded by the rest of my soldiers. Adamma and Tye supported Josh, who wasn't putting any weight on his left leg. A bloody cut traced along Lucia's brow, but she seemed otherwise unscathed.

"Please, Healer Takey," Chan begged. "Please try."

I nodded, closed my eyes, bowed my head, and opened myself. A flood of power poured into me, the familiar colors of my kin and the increasingly less alien white of my soldiers. I felt their uniform desire to do good, to help a fellow pheeworker. It gave me energy.

More than that, it gave me hope. Even with all the support, there was no guarantee I could save Mau. But I had to try.

I took a deep breath and got to work.

"Are you ready?" I called over my shoulder.

Hassan smiled and shook his head. "I never thought I'd see this day."

Standing outside Chan's adobe home, I knew just what he meant. It had only been six days since the standoff between the two armies. Tensions were as high as ever, but there was communication. Both sides had sent envoys and there were talks of a summit to be held at a neutral site. Cordek's ploy had caused damage, no doubt. But it also seemed to have spurred the two races to talk, something that hadn't happened in solars. Both sides knew that the dynamic had changed. The scales had leveled. Humans could pheework. A new reality demanded a new understanding.

But that was work for someone else.

Mau appeared in the doorway, flanked by his mother. The female hadn't left his side since our collective efforts had saved the boy's life. "She's almost ready," Mau managed before his mother shooed him back to bed.

Once the nightroot wore off, the human captives, having been fed a steady diet of dolk milk and jerky, were in surprisingly good shape. It made sense. After all, they represented the base of Cordek's power. I suspected he'd been planning to keep them alive and well for many solars, siphoning their phee whenever he needed it. Regardless, all seven were promptly returned to their families, save for one.

Molly appeared in the doorway, bowed under the weight of a backpack almost as big as she was. She had no family to go home to. "I'm ready!" Molly announced.

Hassan clapped me on the back, positively beaming. "Where are you off to first?"

I winced and rolled my shoulder. At least he hadn't touched my tail. Dalia had bound the broken bones expertly, but it was still sore. "The southern plains," I answered. "Restocking my supplies will give Molly a chance to learn her medicinal plants and spores."

Molly joined us, making a less than pleasant face. "Spores?"

I ignored her and shouldered my pack with a groan. The battle that never was had claimed a single casualty. At some point during our confrontation with Cordek, Aesop, my old dolk, had died on his feet. Perhaps the excitement had been too much for him. Regardless, I was without a wagon or a means to pull it. I didn't mind.

Molly and I would make our way together. We would learn together and learn to work together. With any luck, our peoples would take the same path.

"Come on, Apprentice." I squared my shoulders and started forward. "We've got a long way to go."

Molly fell into step beside me. Chan and his family waved from their doorway. Hassan just smiled.

"Slow and steady," I told Molly. "Slow and steady."

84

ACKNOWLEDGEMENTS

It takes so many people to bring a story to the page and I'm so grateful to all of them. To my beta readers, Richard Van Driesche, Aaron Gaylord, Drew Gaylord, and Cathy Gaylord, thank you for making this story better than it was. To Manthos Lappas, thank you for bringing the world of The Pheeworker's Oath to life with your amazing cover. To Justine, Robert, and the whole Mirror World team, thank you so much for believing in another one of my stories. And to my wife, Hilary, thank you for your unwavering support, love and humor. I couldn't do it without you.

ABOUT THE AUTHOR

Adam Gaylord (he/him) lives in Colorado with a wife that is smarter than him, their two monster children, and a very handsome dog. When not at work as an ecologist, he's usually writing, baking, drawing comics, or some combination thereof. Look him up on GoodReads or find him on Twitter/BlueSky @AuthorGaylord.

To learn more about our authors and our current projects visit: www.mirrorworldpublishing.com, follow @MirrorWorldPub or like us at www.facebook.com/mirrorworldpublishing

Keep reading for a sneak peek at our upcoming new release:

NINE LEVELS

By Elana Gomel

Cleo licked her lips, enjoying the pungent taste of sea salt. The spume flicked her parched skin, peppering it with tiny droplets. Her eyes were filled with a red glow as the sun shone through the closed lids. The warmth was just the right side of heat, thawing out her stiff muscles. Her soaked clothes were slowly drying into a crusty armor.

The bench creaked as somebody heavy sat on the other end of it. Cleo reluctantly unglued her mascara-caked lashes.

The man was indeed big and heavy, so much so that the promenade bench seemed to tilt toward him, lifting Cleo into the air like a child on a seesaw. He sat with his eyes closed, his broad face turned toward the sun. And there was a large spider on his left arm.

She gulped and scooted way, almost falling off the bench. The man did not move. The spider, as big as Cleo's fist, did not move either but its angled legs, haloed with shiny hairs, twitched slightly, showing it was no bizarre decoration or a toy. Its golden head, sunken into its globular body, was peppered with multiple dot-eyes, each swiveling independently of the rest as they focused on Cleo.

She slid off the bench and stood up, her joints creaking and her damp jeans chafing her inner thighs. She rubbed her eyes, disregarding the fact that she was embedding the smears of yesterday's makeup deeper into her tired skin. She blinked, looked back. The spider lazily spread out its legs across the man's tattooed arm. Each leg ended in a small, hooked claw. Its swollen abdomen pulsed with amber highlights.

Okay, so she had been drunk. Okay, so she might have hooked up with a Dutch tourist, which was a mistake - if it had happened. But one thing she was absolutely sure of was that she had not taken any drugs. Her sister's fate was the best guarantee of clean living. So, she had a pint or two occasionally. So, on this Greek vacation she had overdone the combination of retsina, Moscofilero white wine, and the shockingly sweet liqueur called mastika. But it was a vacation, for Christ's sake! Wasn't she entitled to let her hair down a bit? She ran her hand over the stubble on her head, which had dried into a collection of scratchy spikes.

She edged away from the bench, refusing to look back at the big man with his eight-legged pet and walked to the parapet separating the promenade from the beach below. The sugary-white sand glistened in the blinding sunlight that stabbed into Cleo's bruised brain. The indigo wavelets licked at the beach margin scattered with shells. The beach was surprisingly empty: no tourists on tatty towels; no coolers, umbrellas, or kids. And no signs of their impromptu party that started last night when Cleo, Mick, Iris, and a couple of Dutch boys whose names she could not remember had spread their blankets in the balmy Mediterranean night on the shore of Syros.

Had they simply abandoned her and walked back to the hotel? But why? Try as she might, Cleo could not remember anything out of the ordinary except the retsina whose piney taste seemed to take permanent residence in her parched mouth. And why was she soaked? It felt like sometime in the night she had walked into the Aegean fully clothed. Skinny-dipping was one thing, but swimming in your jeans in the midnight sea? And yet, a vague memory, like a disintegrating dream, nibbled at the edges of her mind with images of inky waves, bathwater-warm, embracing her as she swam toward…what?

Cleo squinted into the glare, expecting to see the tawny silhouettes of the smaller Cycladic islands surrounding Syros, but the blue immensity appeared to be empty. Not quite true – there was some vague vertical protrusion on the horizon, shimmering in the sunlight, but the hangover headache suddenly bore into Cleo's temple with such brutal intensity that she gasped and folded down onto the pavement. She kept her eyes shut for a moment and then swiveled away from the sea, subconsciously noting that her dark glasses were apparently gone together with her backpack. At least her credit cards were back at the hotel - if she could make it. Without dark glasses, the flaming July sun in Greece would burn out her blue British eyes and shrivel her damp British brain. Was it what was happening to her? Was she hallucinating giant spiders as a result of a sunstroke?

She climbed to her feet, holding onto the parapet, and looked away from the sea and up, toward the top of the island. Syros was a hilly cone, with the town of Ermoupoli sprawling up the rocky slope. Or at least, that was what it used to be. Because what she was seeing now kicked the golden spider clean out of Cleo's mind.

Instead of the shallow slope dotted with white buildings, an enormous peak rose into the brightness, so tall and so massive that Cleo's brain refused to accept its dimensions. Surely, no mountain outside of Everest could be so large! And the pictures of Everest that Cleo had seen showed a mountain range, craggy summits piled up on top of each other. Here, it was a single symmetrical mount, impossibly large, sticking out of the azure immensity of the sea and dissolving into the cloudless sky. It was as if the modest cone of Syros was somehow stretched up and blown out, creating this geological monstrosity; she could not even see its top.

Cleo realized she was hyperventilating, so she closed her eyes, counted to twenty, and tried to control her breathing. With her Apple watch she could turn on the Breathe app to help her calm down, except her left wrist was bare and her mobile must be in the same place as her backpack, which was nowhere she knew of.

"Are you okay?" a woman's voice asked.

Cleo gratefully turned toward the source of the voice, trying to hang onto reality. But the impossible peak was still there on the margin of her vision, the sunlight piercingly bright on the bands of sage-green vegetation and bare limestone rock.

The woman was middle-aged, with untidy black hair and wearing a bright pink sundress. She reminded Cleo of a magpie or a crow, the way she tilted her head to the left, staring at her with curious round eyes. To Cleo's relief, there were no arachnid pets on, or around, the woman.

"Not really," Cleo confessed, letting go of her stiff upper lip. "I don't know where my phone is, and…."

She realized that her voice was trembling and coughed to save herself the embarrassment of going to pieces in front of a stranger.

"You are dehydrated," the woman declared. "Drink!"

She pulled out a battered metal thermos from her enormous handbag, unscrewed the top, filled it with murky liquid, and gave it to Cleo who stared at it dubiously. She would have expected a plastic bottle, so ubiquitous in Greece that they seemed to generate spontaneously from thin air. But the copper taste in her mouth told her she needed to drink if she was not to pass out. Water was life in the Mediterranean.

She took a long draught. It was water, lukewarm and with a strange aftertaste like ammonia, but at least it was no retsina. Cleo promised herself never to touch anything stronger than lager again.

"Where are you staying?" the woman asked.

"In a tourist hotel. It's called Villa Pharos."

Cleo vaguely pointed toward the end of the promenade where a narrow winding alley led into the huddle of whitewashed buildings. It did not look very familiar, but then, nothing did anymore.

"Come on!" the woman set off at a brisk pace and Cleo, too shocked to assert her independence, followed. She cast a fearful glance toward the bench where she had woken up, but the man with a spider was gone. Had he really been there?

Cleo trudged on, keeping her head down and refusing to look to her right where the impossible monolith of the mountain rose above the promenade. If she did not acknowledge it, would it go away? It was a weird thought but no weirder than everything else that was happening to her. The dazzle of the sun seemed to be dissolving reality into a fluid nightmare. All she wanted right now was to take a hot shower, discard her salt-encrusted clothes, and hide her head under the blanket, hoping to fall asleep – or to wake up.

"Are you alone here?" the crow woman asked.

"With friends."

"Where are they?"

That was a good question, which unleashed Cleo's pent-up indignation at Iris and Mick for abandoning her on the beach. She opened her mouth to say she did not know, and they could go to hell for all she cared – mates didn't do things like this, leaving you alone and unconscious on the beach after a party, to be robbed or worse…

The words stuck in her mouth. She suddenly realized something she should have realized immediately when the crow woman had first addressed her.

Cleo understood the woman perfectly, but she could not tell what language she was speaking.

Cleo spoke fluent Greek. Her mother Daphne was a Greek who married an Englishman named Jerrod Brown and moved to Brighton with him. When Mr. Brown abandoned his wife and twin daughters to disappear into the limbo of deadbeat husbands and fathers, the girls were shipped to their maternal grandmother Eleni on Karystos. When they reluctantly came back to England several years later, Cleo and Cora spoke only Greek to each other. Other identical twins develop their own private languages; the Brown twins picked up the language of Homer for that purpose. Daphne, who always tried to be more British than the Queen, was not happy, but she had enough trouble surviving on the council estate to worry about the twins' national identity.

Growing up bilingual had its advantages and disadvantages. Cora seemed to have accumulated more mental bruises from being suspended between two worlds; Cleo fit in better by learning to shapeshift linguistically, picking up accents like trophies, to the point that her friends in London did not know she spoke Greek, and her Greek acquaintances did not realize she was British.

But even if Cleo had automatically answered the crow woman in Greek, how could she not know what language they were speaking? It made no sense.

"I am Cleo," she said tentatively. "What's your name?"

She heard the sounds leaving her mouth, but for the life of her, she could not say whether it was English or Greek. It was…language; that was all. A means of communication. She understood herself. She knew the crow woman understood her, but it was as if the richness of many different tongues had been compressed into something uniform and bland. Cleo, like all bilingual people, felt she had different personas in Greek and in English. And now these personas were blended into an average

Cleo. As her language became invisible to her, she felt she was becoming invisible to herself.

"I'm Alexandra," the crow woman responded, and Cleo tried to roll the sound of the name on her tongue, tasting each syllable. Was it the broad A of English or the more subdued Ä of Greek? She could not tell.

They dove into the mouth of an alley, and she shivered in the sudden deep shade. As much as Cleo did not want to acknowledge the existence of the mountain, it was hard to do so in this unnatural coolness. In Greece in July, the tiniest patch of shadow was a blessed relief, and most of those were provided by shop awnings and the occasional arcade. Olive trees with their scant foliage begrudged shade to their tenders, but the flank of the mountain, towering above the alley, plunged it into gloom.

She glanced up reluctantly. The mountain was terraced as hillsides in Greece had been for thousands of years. But these terraces were enormous. She started counting. One, two…

The crow woman stopped in front of a chipped blue door set into the white wall.

"Villa Pharos," she declared.

Cleo wanted to say that it did not look right, but the words stuck in her mouth.

Above the wall was a painted sign with the name of the establishment. But instead of Greek letters, the sign was covered with twitching spiders.

This book is coming soon!

Follow our blog, newsletter, Facebook Page or website for updates.

We are an independent publishing house based in Windsor, Ontario. We publish quality paperbacks and ebooks that feature other worlds, times and versions of reality. Our novels are for all ages and are creative, unique, imaginative and engaging.

We pride ourselves on our originality and 'outside the box' thinking, while taking a good look at the question, 'what if?' Our stories are never ordinary, the dialogue and action engaging, the characters believable, and there will always be some element of romance, adventure, science or magic. We are dedicated to bring our readers novels that will not only entertain them, but also teach them something about the world they live in by showing them one that mirrors it. We hope you'll consider picking up a novel from our collection today so you can see for yourself what we're all about.

You'll find a wide variety of our wonderful titles in our online bookstore and you can also purchase or review them through most major retailers worldwide.To learn more about our authors and our current projects visit: www.mirrorworldpublishing.com or follow @MirrorWorldPub or like us at www.facebook.com/mirrorworldpublishing

www.ingramcontent.com/pod-product-compliance
Lightning Source LLC
Chambersburg PA
CBHW021559310726
48972CB00003B/868